FOLLOW THE CODES . . .

Join Art and Camille in viewing famous paintings—all portals to Art's memory and identity—with the interactive QR code feature you'll discover in these pages.

To access the paintings you will need a smartphone or tablet and a connection to the Internet. If you don't have a QR reader app on your device, ask a parent or guardian to download a free QR reader from the app store. Once you have downloaded the app, simply open it and hover the device over the QR code, which looks like this:

The art will appear in your browser.

If you don't have access to a smartphone or tablet, be sure to visit www.nga.gov to view many of the paintings mentioned in this book. Happy sleuthing!

The Van Gogh DECEPTION

The Van Gogh DECEPTION

by
Deron Hicks

HOUGHTON MIFFLIN HARCOURT

BOSTON NEW YORK

www.hmhco.com

The text was set in Weiss.

The Library of Congress has cataloged the hardcover edition as follows:
Names: Hicks, Deron R., author.
Title: The Van Gogh deception / Deron R. Hicks.
Description: Boston ; New York : Houghton Mifflin Harcourt, [2017] | Summary: "When a young boy is discovered in Washington, DC's National Gallery of Art without any recollection of who he is, he must piece together the disjointed clues of his origins while using his limited knowledge to stop one of the greatest art frauds ever attempted" —Provided by publisher.
Identifiers: LCCN 2016010019
Subjects: | CYAC: Mystery and detective stories. | National Gallery of Art (U.S.)—Fiction. | Art—Forgeries—Fiction. | Identity—Fiction. | Memory—Fiction. | Washington (D.C.)—Fiction. | BISAC: JUVENILE FICTION / Mysteries & Detective Stories. | JUVENILE FICTION / Art & Architecture. | JUVENILE FICTION / Action & Adventure / General. | JUVENILE FICTION / Social Issues / Friendship.
Classification: LCC PZ7.H531615 Van 2017 | DDC [Fic]—dc23
LC record available at https://lccn.loc.gov/2016010019

ISBN: 978-0-544-75927-5 hardcover
ISBN: 978-1-328-63517-4 paperback

Printed in the United States of America
DOC 10 9 8 7 6 5
4500756060

To my parents, for all their love and support.
To my wife, Angela, for her persistence and patience.
To my children, Meg and Parker, because they
inspire me every day.

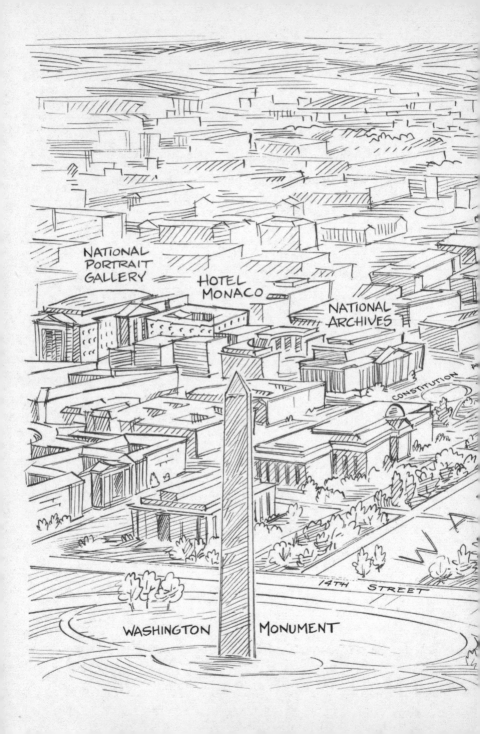

UNITED STATES CAPITOL

NATIONAL GALLERY of ART

NATIONAL GALLERY WEST WING

WASHINGTON MALL

INDEPENDENCE AVE

J. MATHISON

PROLOGUE

The boy appeared out of nowhere.

He could see the boy's reflection in the protective glass that surrounded the small sculpture. The boy was blond—his hair a bit unruly, but otherwise normal-looking. He wore a blue jacket and sneakers.

He tried not to stare directly at the boy—it seemed rude, under the circumstances. Nobody likes to be stared at, particularly by a stranger. So he watched from the corner of his eye as the boy glanced around the room.

Maybe the boy was looking for someone? Perhaps his parents?

The room was filled with famous paintings and sculptures. The boy, however, didn't seem to notice. The crowd swirled about the room, but the boy just sat on the bench, his hands in his lap and a blank expression on his face.

It was hard to say how long he sat there watching the boy—he wasn't wearing a watch, and there wasn't a clock in the room. It was strange: time seemed to stand still. Had he been there an hour? Two hours? Longer?

No one seemed to notice the boy—no one but him.

Everyone else just passed through the room as if the boy didn't exist, or was invisible.

He worried about the boy. He seemed lost.

Who was he?

Why was he here?

Rude or not, he couldn't help but stare.

He glanced down briefly at his own blue jacket and his own sneakers. Odd, he thought—so much like the boy in the reflection.

He looked back up at the boy. He wanted to speak. He wanted to tell the boy that everything would be all right. But he couldn't find the words. The boy simply stared back at him.

He felt powerless to help.

And so he waited—hoping someone might come along and help the lost boy sitting on the bench.

PART 1

"We must make an effort like the lost, like the desperate."

—letter from Vincent van Gogh to his brother Theo,
2 April 1881

CHAPTER 1

For almost three hundred years, the simple stone structures on the outskirts of the small French village of Locro-
nan had served as home to a family of farmers. The largest
barn, constructed of thick blocks of local granite, had once
housed the family's small collection of livestock but no longer served that purpose. Victor Baudin was no farmer and
had converted the family barn to suit his unique profession. The well-worn stone pavers, the plastered walls, the
thick wood beams, and the faint smell of hay and manure
remained. However, bright fluorescent lights, modern windows, and a new central heating and air-conditioning system—with silver vents slithering around the ceiling of the
former barn—made it clear that this was no longer a home
to poultry, cows, and goats.

Along one long wall ran several shelves. One shelf—
stretching up to the full height of the ceiling—was lined
with dark bottles of boiled oil, vinegar, bleach, gallotannic

acid, ink of cuttlefish, hydrochloric acid, elemental mercury, and rainwater. The next shelf was filled with tins. A crisp white label identified the contents of each: carbonate of lead, zinc oxide, sulfide of mercury, ground mollusk shells, hydrate of iron, flaxseed, realgar, dragon's blood, powdered mummy, and lapis lazuli.

A large industrial oven sat at the far end of the room between two wide wooden drying racks, and a long metal table ran down the middle of the former barn. The stark industrial appearance of the oven and the table contrasted sharply with the rough stone structure in which they were housed. Bunsen burners, microscopes, beakers of every conceivable size and shape, a condenser, a mortar and pestle, clamps, and tubing had been shoved to one side of the table. Beneath the table were rows of tall wooden boxes with handwritten labels such as "filbert," "hake," "badger," "mottler," "mongoose," and "cat's tongue." The other half of the table was empty except for one item—Baudin's greatest creation.

Victor Baudin had often joked to himself that in another day and age the room would have been perfectly suited for the work of an alchemist or a sorcerer. While there was far more science than witchcraft in his efforts, the room did not lack in its share of wizardry.

Baudin turned to the table to examine his masterpiece once more. As always, there was an odd combination of pride, relief, and sadness when he finished a project. His client—a man he had never met and whose name had never been offered or asked for—had been remarkably patient. Three years, Baudin had explained. Even with modern technology there were certain methods—ancient techniques—that could not be rushed or duplicated. The client had accepted Baudin's terms, paid the bills in cash as they came due, and waited for the news that the job was finished. And now it was, and as close to perfect as it could be. The client would be pleased.

The knock on the barn door startled the old man out of his reverie. He quickly covered his work with a light cotton cloth.

Presentation mattered.

"Un moment," he yelled as he made his way across the room.

He drew back a creaky iron bolt and pulled open the heavy oak door. A short, balding man with a bushy mustache stood outside. The cold winter wind whipped through the open door.

"Come in, come in," said Baudin. *"Il fait froid."*

The man stepped inside. Baudin bolted the door back in place and turned to greet his visitor.

"Your work is finished?" the balding man asked. Although the visitor tried to hide it, Baudin could hear the excitement in the man's voice.

"Yes," replied the old man. "Your client will be pleased."

Baudin pointed to the far end of the room. *"Suivez-moi,"* he said. Follow me.

The men made their way across the room to the far end of the metal table.

"Gracier les dramatics," said Baudin as he took hold of one corner of the cloth that covered his creation. "I thought it deserved a proper introduction."

The balding man smiled and nodded approvingly. "Of course."

The old man removed the cloth with a flourish and stepped aside. The balding man gasped, then quickly regained his composure. He pulled a pair of reading glasses from his coat pocket and bent over Baudin's creation. He spent several minutes examining the front and then turned it on its side. He ran his finger across the back of the creation. He held his index finger up for the old man to see.

"Dust," the balding man said appreciatively.

Baudin nodded. *"Les détails sont importants,"* he replied. The details are important.

The balding man laid the creation back down and bent over it once more. For several minutes he said nothing. Finally, he turned back to the old man.

"Fingernail?" he asked.

"Yes," replied Baudin.

The balding man ran the edge of his nail on his right index finger across a small corner of the creation. He bent over and examined the area. His fingernail had not left a mark or impression.

The balding man stood up, put his reading glasses back in his pocket, and turned to the old man.

"The materials conform?" he asked. "No substitutes? Everything's authentic?"

"As your client required," said Baudin.

"The paperwork?"

Baudin retrieved a large folder from a side table and presented it to the balding man. The balding man quickly thumbed through the folder.

"Everything appears to be in order," he said.

Baudin opened the oven. Heat blasted into the room. The balding man placed the folder on one of the racks and closed the door. The men stood silently and watched. Within seconds the paper had burst into flames. Two minutes later only ashes remained.

The balding man turned to Baudin. "And the others?" he asked.

Baudin pointed to the drying racks, which were stacked high with more creations. "On schedule," he said.

The balding man nodded and turned back to the table. "It is truly a masterpiece," he said appreciatively.

Baudin smiled. It *was* a masterpiece. The alchemist had indeed turned lead into gold.

CHAPTER 2

10:37 p.m.
Thursday, December 14
Parking garage, Washington, DC

He had done everything he could.

The tall middle-aged man took one last glance at his phone. Cell service was almost nonexistent in the below-ground parking garage, but he still checked. The phone confirmed what he already knew: NO SERVICE, the small letters read at the top left corner of the screen. The phone and the information it contained were now a liability. He scrolled through the phone's settings and found the Reset button. Within seconds everything he had ever saved on his phone —contacts, emails, photographs . . . everything—was gone. The man slipped the phone back into his coat pocket.

There were only two cars in the massive concrete space: his small rental and a large black SUV parked in front of the only vehicle exit. It would take far more than wishful thinking for his small car to have any chance of pushing that behemoth out of the way. Good thing leaving in the car was not part of the man's plan.

He glanced across the parking garage at the door leading to the elevators. A large man wearing a black winter coat now blocked the entrance.

There was only one other way out of the garage — a service door leading back into the building. Getting there was the problem. The parking garage was L shaped. The man would have to make it to a concrete pillar fifty or so feet away, turn right around the corner, and then it was another hundred feet to the service entrance. In his youth, he might have had a chance. But not now. There was no way he could make it to the door before he was caught. But making it to the door wasn't the point. He just needed to buy a little time. He adjusted the satchel on his shoulder.

The rear door of the SUV opened and a man stepped out.

"Just hand it over," the newcomer yelled across the garage, "and you'll be free to go." His voice echoed across the empty concrete space.

The middle-aged man wanted to laugh. There was no way he would ever be allowed to go free. He'd be lucky to make it through the rest of the night alive. But he didn't panic. There was too much at stake. He backed up against the trunk of his rental car and took a deep breath. It was time.

He knocked once — ever so lightly — on the back of the car. He then took his satchel in his hand and started walking as quickly as he could toward the large concrete pillar. All he needed to do was make it to the pillar and around the corner by the count of twenty.

1, 2, 3, 4, he slowly counted to himself as he walked.

"Don't make this difficult!" the man standing by the SUV yelled.

He ignored the man and continued to walk. He was almost halfway to the pillar.

5, 6, 7, 8, 9 . . .

The man in the black coat, who'd been stationed at the elevators, started walking toward him.

10, 11, 12, 13 . . .

Twenty feet to go.

The SUV revved its engine in the distance behind him. He glanced over his shoulder. The vehicle was now moving swiftly across the garage to intercept him. He started sprinting.

14, 15, 16, 17 . . .

Three more seconds. He had to make it around the corner in three more seconds or none of this would matter. He could hear footsteps behind him. The man in the black coat was closing the distance faster than expected. The middle-aged man needed to pick up the pace.

18 . . .

19 . . .

He could hear the footsteps getting closer.

. . . 20!

He made it to the concrete pillar, pivoted to his right, and headed toward the service entrance. Time was now on his side, but every additional second mattered.

He could hear the man's footsteps almost directly behind him now. He whipped around and threw his heavy leather satchel at his pursuer's feet. He had intended merely to use it as a distraction—to gain a little more time and a little more distance—but the satchel hit the man flush on his right shin and sent him cursing and sprawling to the concrete.

Maybe, the middle-aged man thought, he could actually make it to the service door. Once inside, he could contact the police. Maybe everything would work out.

BAM.

A gunshot followed by an explosion of concrete brought him back to reality. The bullet has missed him by mere inches, but shards of concrete had slashed across his neck above his collar. He could feel warm blood flowing down his back. He stopped and looked to his left. The man from the SUV was now standing less than thirty feet away and pointing a gun directly at him. He seemed incredibly young.

"No more games," the man said.

The middle-aged man knew there was no sense in continuing to run. He dropped his arms to his side and leaned back against the wall.

"Where is it?" the young man demanded.

The middle-aged man took a deep breath. "Where is what?"

The young man smiled. "I know why you came here tonight."

"I don't know what you are talking about."

The young man sighed. "Very well, we'll do this the hard way."

The young man motioned toward the man in the black coat — the same man who had been knocked to the ground with the satchel, who was now getting to his feet.

"Take care of him," the young man said.

"My pleasure," the man in the black coat replied.

CHAPTER 3

4:53 p.m.
Friday, December 15
West Building, National Gallery of Art,
Washington, DC

A tall white-haired man in a dark blue blazer sat down next to the boy.

"It's closing time, pal," the man said. "We need to find your parents."

The man had a kind voice.

The boy looked up. "I know," he said quietly.

"My name's Ken Johnson," the man said. He held out his hand to the boy, who shook it.

"I'm a docent at the museum," the man explained. "I help people. The security guard said you've been sitting here for quite a while. I'm sure your parents are worried."

The boy turned and looked at the famous sculpture by Edgar Degas — a young dancer sculpted in wax, her eyes closed and chin lifted, her hands entwined behind her back. The boy didn't respond. He didn't have the words to respond.

"Do you know where your parents are?" Johnson asked. His voice was calm and reassuring.

"No," the boy said. His eyes never left the sculpture.

"Tell you what," said Johnson. "Give me your name, and we'll track them down for you, okay?"

"My name?"

"Yes," said Johnson, "your name?"

The boy turned and looked at him. "I don't know my name."

7:07 p.m.
Friday, December 15
First District Station, Metropolitan Police
Department, Washington, DC

The boy sat in a chair and stared at a TV on a beat-up credenza. The office was small and hot. He could hear air whistling through a vent in the ceiling. One of the detectives had brought him to the room ten minutes or so ago and asked him to wait. There was little to do other than sit and stare at the television. SpongeBob SquarePants was dancing around silently on the screen. The boy had muted the TV. He wasn't in the mood for SpongeBob's annoying laugh.

A social worker had picked up the boy at the museum

and taken him to the hospital. The doctor in the emergency room had been nice—he spoke with a soft Jamaican accent and had thick dreadlocks. He had asked a lot of questions, but the boy had few answers. He felt bad about that, but he just didn't remember anything. He had no idea when he had arrived at the museum, why he was there, who he was, who his parents were, or where he lived. The doctor had checked for any sign of a blow to the head or some other injury that might explain the memory loss. Nothing. Another doctor —a thin, bald man who seemed in a hurry—had come in and spoken with the boy briefly. He wasn't nearly as nice as the doctor with the Jamaican accent and dreadlocks. The new doctor was a neurologist—a brain doctor, the nice doctor had explained. The new doctor—the not-so-nice one—had diagnosed him with a type of amnesia caused by a traumatic event. The nice doctor had told him there was not much they could do for him—that his memory would return when he was ready for it to return. The nice doctor had given him a pat on the shoulder, told him to hang in there, and then left.

Patrick Star had now joined SpongeBob on the screen. They danced silently around the bottom of the ocean on the TV.

Despite the almost oppressive heat in the room, the boy didn't remove his jacket. It was all he had—a blue zip-up he had been wearing when he was found. Written on the tag on the inside of the jacket was the name Arthur. The people at the hospital had asked if that was his name, but the boy didn't know. The name didn't sound familiar to him. The jacket could have been a hand-me-down or someone else's jacket that he had borrowed or picked up along the way.

There was a knock on the door, and a woman with dark, shortly cropped hair stuck her head inside. She had a pair of glasses hanging from a chain around her neck.

"My name's Detective Evans," she said. "May I come in?"

The boy simply nodded. It wasn't as if he could say no.

The detective pulled over a chair from the other side of the small office and sat down directly in front of the boy. She placed a folder in her lap and opened it. He could see his photo stapled on the inside of the file along with the report from the emergency room. And even though the folder was upside down, he could also see the word "runaway" and a question mark written in dark ink across the inside cover. The detective caught him looking at the file and quickly closed it.

"I've been asked to sit down and talk with you a bit," the detective said. She seemed nice enough, but he could see that she was watching him closely.

"Any luck remembering your name?" she asked.

The boy shook his head. "No."

"My son has blond hair and green eyes just like you," she said. "I sure would miss him if he disappeared. Do you know where your parents are?"

"No," the boy responded.

The detective's eyes never left his face.

"Do you know their names?" she asked.

"No."

"Do you know your address?"

"No."

"Do you live in Washington, DC?"

"I don't know."

"How old are you?"

The boy paused. That was a good question.

"Twelve — I think," he replied. "But I'm not sure."

"Do you know how you got to the museum?"

The boy mulled over the question.

"No," he finally replied. "I was just there."

The detective gestured toward the TV. "Whatcha watching?" she asked.

"*SpongeBob SquarePants.*"

"My son loves that show," she said. "I think it's kind of silly. Do you like it?"

"It's okay," the boy responded.

"You remember SpongeBob, but you can't remember your name?"

The boy shook his head. "I can't," he said apologetically.

The detective put on her glasses, opened the folder, and scribbled a few notes.

"Can I ask you a question?" the boy asked.

"Of course." The detective looked up from the file.

"Do you think I'm telling the truth?"

The detective closed the folder and leaned back in her chair.

"I'll be honest with you," she said. "The chief detective asked me to interview you because . . . well . . . I'm really good at getting to the truth. I read people. I look for the little signs that someone isn't telling the truth — lack of eye contact, too much blinking, hand movements, shifting in the seat — stuff people don't even realize they're doing."

"Did you read me?" the boy asked.

"I did," replied the detective.

She paused.

"I think you're telling the truth," she finally said. "And I'm going to do everything I can do to help you find out who you are."

The boy nodded. He liked Detective Evans.

Mary Sullivan checked in with the duty officer and then took a seat in the waiting room of the police station. She had learned long ago that patience was an absolute requirement for being a foster parent. Her job — she was a senior editor for a book publisher in New York — afforded her a certain level of flexibility. She always had plenty of work to do, but her job gave her the ability to work from home and on a schedule largely of her choosing — even if that meant poring over a manuscript at two in the morning.

She was used to the late-night calls and the sudden need for the temporary placement of a child. The children ultimately moved on to relatives or long-term placement in another community. Mary had developed a reputation for handling difficult situations—children with severe physical disabilities, children who had suffered abuse at the hands of a parent, children who had simply been abandoned under the worst of circumstances. This situation, however, was unlike any she had ever encountered.

She had been on the way to pick up her daughter when she received the call from social services. Another lesson she had learned long ago: calls always came when she least expected them. They had asked if she could pick up a child who needed temporary placement. She had initially declined—she had a pile of manuscripts on her desk at home that were screaming to be reviewed, and Christmas was less than two weeks away. But the social worker had explained the situation and begged her to help. Mary had reluctantly agreed.

The door leading into the back offices of the police station opened, and out walked Detective Brooke Evans. She was accompanied by a boy, perhaps eleven or twelve years of age, with shaggy blond hair and green eyes.

"Thank you for coming," said Detective Evans. "It's good to see you again."

Mary looked the boy directly in his eyes. He was every bit as tall as she was. "Happy to be here," she replied to the detective. Extending her hand to the boy, she said, "I'm Mary Sullivan."

The boy took her hand and shook it. "Am I going home with you, Ms. Sullivan?" he asked.

Mary smiled. The boy seemed well mannered, which was a good sign. "Yes," she said. "And please, call me Mary."

The boy nodded. "I don't have any clothes," he said. "Or a toothbrush. I really should brush my teeth. It's getting late."

"Don't worry," said Mary. "I think I can handle a toothbrush and a clean set of clothes." She turned to Detective Evans. "Any leads?"

The detective shook her head. "Not yet. According to the security tape at the museum, he had been sitting in that room for most of the day. I'll call you as soon as I know something. Being this close to Christmas, I suspect his parents will show up soon."

Detective Evans turned to the boy and placed her hand on his shoulder. "Be good for Mary," she said.

"I will," the boy assured her.

Detective Evans watched as the boy and Mary left the precinct.

The whole situation was odd.

There was, of course, the possibility that the boy was faking. She couldn't discount it entirely. She had been wrong before—every detective makes mistakes. But everything about the boy suggested that he was telling the truth.

It was as if he had just appeared out of thin air in the National Gallery of Art.

CHAPTER 4

7:35 p.m.
Friday, December 15
Parking lot, Washington, DC

"Where do you live?" asked the boy. It seemed a reasonable question. He didn't know what else to say, and he felt as though he needed to say something.

"North of here, near Dupont Circle—not far," Mary Sullivan said as she opened the rear passenger-side door of her vehicle—a dark blue Honda CR-V—and pushed a large pile of clothes, schoolbooks, and papers to the middle of the row.

The boy took a seat next to the mound of items in the back. "How long will I be staying with you?" he asked as he buckled his seat belt.

"Let's start with tonight and go from there," said Mary.

"Okay," the boy replied. That seemed fair.

Mary started the car and headed toward the exit of the parking lot.

"Just one quick stop before we get home," said Mary. "I need to pick up my daughter from my sister's house."

"How old's your daughter?" asked the boy.

"Ten," she replied. "But she thinks she's thirty."

"What's her name?"

"Camille," said Mary.

"Camille," the boy repeated. "Nice name."

"Thanks," replied Mary. "I'm partial to it myself."

The vehicle pulled out of the lot and onto the street. A light snow was starting to fall.

"Supposed to get cold tonight," said Mary. "I bet the snow sticks."

The boy did not respond. He simply stared out the window at the snow flickering through the glow of the streetlights.

After driving for about twenty minutes in silence, Mary pulled up in front of a small brick home and beeped once. A tall woman with jet black hair peeked out the front door of the house and waved at the car. Mary rolled down her window and waved back.

"Sorry for being late," she called. "How's she been?"

"She's been Camille," the woman called back.

"Sorry!" Mary replied.

The tall woman opened the front door wide, and a short girl carrying a large pink book bag and bundled up in a thick jacket, rubber boots, and a wool cap exploded out of the house and ran toward the car.

"Thanks, Aunt Judy," the girl hollered over her shoulder. She opened the rear door, tossed her book bag onto the floorboard, and plopped into the row with the boy. The large mound of clothes, schoolbooks and papers separated them.

"Hello," said the girl. "Who are you?"

Mary interrupted before he could respond. "He's staying with us tonight," she explained.

The girl took off her wool cap, and a large mane of red woolly hair exploded out. The boy didn't think she looked anything like her mom, who had dark brown hair pulled neatly into a bun on the back of her head. The girl extended her hand to the boy over the pile that divided them. "I'm Camille," she said. Her voice was friendly and welcoming.

The boy shook her hand. "Hi."

"And what's your name?" prompted Camille.

"I'm not sure," said the boy.

"What's that supposed to mean?" asked Camille. "You gotta have a name."

"He has amnesia," said Mary. "That means he can't—"

"I know what amnesia means," Camille replied sharply.

"Just give him a break from Hurricane Camille, okay?"

"But that is so cool!" exclaimed Camille, completely ignoring her mother. "I've never met anyone with amnesia. We've had lots of kids stay with us, but nobody with amnesia. I forgot my locker combination one time at school, but it was only the second week of class so that's probably why. I don't think it was amnesia, but you never know. So what's it like? Can you remember anything?"

She held up three fingers before the boy could answer. "Do you know how many fingers this is?"

She paused for a second, then leaned over the pile between them and stared intently at the boy.

"Do you even know what fingers are?" she asked. She wiggled her fingers in front of his face. "Or numbers?"

"I know what fingers are," the boy said. "And you held up three of them."

There was a slightly defensive tone in his voice.

"Christmas is almost here," said Camille. "Do you remember Christmas?"

"C'mon," interrupted Mary. "Give him a break—he's had a rough day."

Camille once again ignored her mother. "Well, what am I supposed to call you?" she asked. "I could call you Theo. I once had a turtle named Theo. He wasn't very exciting but I liked him. He died. Mom said it was because I didn't change his water, or feed him, or something like that. He smelled real, real bad. We took him out to a pond and tried to set him free, but when I put him into the water, he just sank. Plop. Straight down. To the bottom. No bubbles or anything. Just plop and down. But I liked him."

"You can't name him after your dead turtle," said Mary.

Camille turned to the boy. "But you don't know what your name is, do you?"

"No," he conceded.

Camille turned then to her mother. "And I can't just call

26

him nothing, can I?" she said. "And his name might be Theo — or Bill, Buster, Scooter, or Red. It could be anything. Red would also be kinda cool — or Hank. I've always liked that name. Hank."

"There's a name on my jacket," the boy said. "Arthur."

"Arthur?" exclaimed Camille. "What kind of name is that? Sounds like a butler or some old man."

The boy's face turned red with embarrassment. "I don't even know if it's my name," he said quietly. "I can't remember."

Camille paused and considered the situation.

"Don't get me wrong — Arthur's not that bad," she finally said. "And maybe we could call you Artie, or Art. That's short for Arthur, isn't it?"

"I guess so," he replied.

"Well?" Camille asked her mother. "Can I call him Art?"

"It's up to him."

Camille turned to the boy. "How 'bout it?"

"I guess it's better than being named after a dead turtle."

Camille burst out laughing.

"Fine," said Mary. "Art it is. Now let's get on home and eat supper. I'm famished, and it's late."

Camille looked across the back seat at the boy. "It's spaghetti night," she said excitedly. "I love spaghetti night."

A slight smile creased the boy's face. "I like spaghetti. At least I think I do."

* * *

27

Dorchek Palmer stood in the dark in the middle of the living room of the small carriage house apartment. He was twenty-eight years old but could have easily passed for sixteen. He had a mop of unruly light brown hair and stood just five feet five inches tall. People tended to look past him, assuming he was just some high school or college kid, which was fine by him. By the time he had turned twenty-five, he had made tens of millions of dollars developing game apps for smartphones and consulting for some of the largest technology firms in the world. But developing game apps and consulting — as rich as it may have made him — was not exactly the life he had envisioned for himself. Palmer was a thrill seeker, and he used his millions to finance a life of adventure — mountain climbing in Nepal, running the Marathon des Sables, swimming with great whites in Australia, BASE jumping from Angel Falls. He tried everything at least once — the more dangerous, the better. But eventually he grew bored — risking life and limb simply wasn't enough. He needed something big — something beyond anything he or anyone else had ever attempted. And then, one day in Paris as he was walking along the Rue de Rivoli next to the abandoned palace of Louis XIV, the scheme had come

28

to him in a flash. He immediately rejected the idea as crazy —too risky for even his tastes. But he eventually realized that it was exactly what he needed—something so risky that it scared even him. And it was this new undertaking —an experience unlike anything he or anyone else had ever conceived—that had brought him to this small apartment in the dark of night.

Palmer pushed the button on the side of his watch to illuminate the time. It was getting late, but he knew that there would not be any sleep tonight. Events had taken an unexpected turn the night before, and the stakes had increased significantly—the spider was loose in the city.

This was not, Palmer had reminded his team, the time to panic. The mission had to proceed—obstacles had to be overcome. But the fact remained that unless they could locate the spider within the next two days, years of effort would prove worthless.

Palmer did not intend to let that happen.

A member of Palmer's team had spent the entire day watching the small apartment from across the street. To Palmer's surprise, no one had shown up. Palmer knew it was risky, but they had to search the apartment. Time was running out, and, although there was no guarantee that they would even find what they were looking for, they had to make sure it wasn't here. Maybe they would get lucky, but Palmer doubted it.

"Windows secure?" Palmer said aloud.

A short, thin man dressed entirely in black used a small flashlight to check the seal on the thick cloth that covered the window in the kitchen. The edges of the cloth were backed with a strong adhesive that attached securely to the wall surrounding the casement. Similar cloths covered the rest of the windows in the apartment.

"All secure," the man said.

"Doors?" asked Palmer.

"Secure," another man said.

Palmer and his team had made it inside the apartment and secured the windows and doors within three minutes. His team consisted of only five members, but they were the best money could buy. They were professionals from across the globe who had been highly trained in covert operations. Specialists in electronic surveillance, computer technology, alarm systems, and night operations, they broke into places that were never supposed to be broken into. Every member of his team spoke at least three languages, three were pilots, and all were experts with a wide variety of weapons. They could blend into almost any environment and survive almost any challenge. They were dangerous people who had spent their careers in dangerous situations. And they were also highly paid, which ensured a reasonable measure of loyalty.

"Lights on in three," said Palmer as he removed his night-vision goggles. The two other men followed suit. At the count of three, Palmer flicked the switch in the living room. Bright light flooded the room.

"Any light bleed outside?" asked Palmer. The small communication device in his ear transmitted his question to another team member stationed outside as a lookout.

A moment later a woman's voice crackled through the device. "No bleed," the voice said. "All dark."

"Clear?" asked Palmer.

"Residents of main house have not returned," said the voice in his ear. "No sign of anyone else. All clear."

"We're secure," said Palmer. He checked his watch again. "Top to bottom. Five minutes, no longer."

The two members of the team who had accompanied Palmer inside proceeded to search every drawer in every room in the small nondescript apartment. They did so quickly and precisely, disturbing nothing and leaving no trace. Every book and magazine was opened, examined, and returned to its original location. The small area rug in the living room was pulled up, turned over, and then put back in place. The covers of every light switch and electrical outlet were removed and the boxes examined. The mattress on the bed and the pillows on the couch were patted down. Everything in the small apartment was opened up, turned over, and otherwise thoroughly examined. And everything in the small apartment was returned to the exact location in which it had been found.

Palmer slowly made his way through the house. He ran his hand across the top of every door. He removed every floor vent, wall vent, and ceiling vent. He checked the refrigerator. He checked the freezer. He checked the small closet that served as a pantry and every can, bottle, and bag in it. He tried to think of everywhere and anywhere it could be hidden. His job was to make sure every single part of the search protocol was followed and that nothing was missed. And despite his youth, the two men on his team — both at least a decade older than he was — knew he was good at his job. He had to be. The business at hand did not allow for mistakes.

"Report," Palmer called out.

"Negative," both of the men replied.

They located a laptop in the bedroom. It did not prove terribly difficult to get into — it had taken Palmer all of about thirty seconds to find a back door around the password. A quick glance at the files on the hard drive did not reveal anything particularly interesting — mostly personal stuff. His team would, of course, take the computer, and Palmer would examine it more thoroughly on his own time, along with the smartphone they had retrieved the previous night. But Palmer didn't have high hopes for what he would find on either the phone or the laptop, and the rest of the apartment did not appear any more promising.

Palmer knew that searching the apartment had simply

been an effort to cover all their bases. The truth was, they knew who could bring the spider to them.

Find the boy, and they would find the spider.

But the boy had already slipped through their fingers once. And now he had managed to elude them for almost twenty-four hours. As far as they could tell, the boy had not gone to the police, which had been surprising given the circumstances of his escape. Palmer, however, had arranged a contingency plan in the event the police became involved.

Two days to find the spider.

Palmer checked his watch. It was time to go. He placed a small video transmitter above one of the windows in the living room so he could continue to monitor the apartment. He then called the two men into the living room. One of them handed him the laptop.

"Everything still clear outside?" Palmer asked.

"All clear," the voice in his ear responded.

"Lights out in ten," said Palmer, "then clear the covers and let's get out of here."

The men nodded. They put their night-vision goggles back on and prepared for the darkness.

Palmer took one last look around the apartment. He sensed that something wasn't right about the whole setup. The apartment was too normal, too neat.

He turned off the light switch.

The small apartment was dark once again.

* * *

"Time for bed," said Mary Sullivan. "It's getting late."

Camille placed her book on the nightstand. She loved reading mysteries, and this particular mystery about Shakespeare was great. But there was no sense in arguing with her mother. It was already well past her normal bedtime, and besides, she could feel herself starting to drift.

Mary sat on the edge of Camille's bed. "So what do you think?" her mother asked. "Of the boy?"

"He's nice," said Camille. "Doesn't talk much, though. He barely said anything all night."

Mary paused. "He's lost," she finally said. "He doesn't know who he is or where he came from — and it's almost Christmas. That has to be hard."

Camille nodded. She couldn't imagine being away from her mother at Christmastime. "Maybe he's a spy," Camille suggested. "You know, some sort of secret agent or something. There're all kinds of those people in Washington, DC."

Mary smiled. "Don't let your imagination get the best of you. He's just a kid, like you. And he has parents out there somewhere who are worried about him."

"I suppose," Camille said as she snuggled deep under her

covers. "But being a spy would be way cooler." She could feel her eyelids growing heavy.

"He needs a friend," said Mary. "Someone who will look out for him. Can you do that for me?"

"I always do," replied Camille sleepily.

Mary kissed her daughter lightly on the forehead. "I don't know what happened to him," she said, "but he needs to know that he's safe with us."

"I'll watch out for him," said Camille. Her words were faint and slurred—her eyes closed. "I promise." A moment later she was deeply asleep.

CHAPTER 5

He came upon a tall gate — cast iron with patches of rust, and cobwebs strung between its thick metal pickets. The gate swung ever so slightly in the wind, creaking as it made its way back and forth on ancient pins.

It was late, and the shadows had grown deep and long. The bright colors of the day had faded into gray.

He turned to head back the way he had come, but night had overtaken him. The path was now dark and uncertain.

He could feel his heart beating in his chest.

He had been here before, but he couldn't remember what happened or which way to go.

He called out for help, but there was no reply. He was alone.

There was nowhere to go but forward.

The gate was ajar — the path beyond, uncertain.

6:30 a.m.
Saturday, December 16
Sullivan residence, Washington, DC

The boy sat straight up in bed.

He tried desperately to hold on to the dream, but it slipped from his memory.

Faint images were all that remained, the afterglow of something real. It was like trying to grab smoke.

The doctor at the hospital had told the boy not to get frustrated. The memories would come back when he was ready, the doctor had explained. So the boy held on to his dreams. They weren't much—and they were weird—but they were more than what he'd had yesterday.

He glanced over at the small clock by the bed— 6:31 a.m.

It was strange. He still couldn't remember his name, where he was from, or who his parents were. He knew nothing about himself. But he knew exactly where he was at this precise moment—the home of Mary Sullivan and her ten-year-old daughter, Camille. He remembered every detail from the night before. He remembered arriving at the home that Mary and Camille Sullivan shared—a narrow three-story white-brick house squeezed into the middle of a block of red-brick homes. He remembered listening to Camille go on and on about her pet turtle, Theo, as her mother prepared dinner. He remembered diving into a large plate of spaghetti, feeling as if he hadn't eaten for days. He remembered the long, hot shower before bed. He remembered climbing into the tall bed in the guest room, sinking into the soft, thick mattress, and falling immediately to sleep.

And that's what made it so frustrating. Everything from the past twelve hours was so vivid. But before that? Nothing but vague memories from a dream. It was as if he had simply popped into existence yesterday afternoon at the museum. He had no idea who he really was. Was he one of those kids —like Camille—who talked nonstop about everything? Or was he quiet and shy? Did he have a bad temper, or did things just roll off his back? Was he bothered by little things, like people chewing gum too loudly or the sound of potato chips crunching in a bag? Did he have lots of friends, or was he a loner? Was he a good student? Did he like sports, or was he more into video games? What type of music did he like?

There were so many questions—and absolutely no answers.

The boy lay down and tried to sleep, but it was useless. His brain was working overtime—his thoughts raced along at a mile a minute, trying to make sense of the small clues provided during his sleep.

He sat back up, turned on the lamp beside his bed, and listened for any sign that someone else was awake— he didn't feel right about wandering around the house by himself.

It didn't take long. Almost immediately he heard someone walking around on the first floor. The boy jumped out of bed and headed downstairs.

He found Mary pouring herself a cup of coffee in the kitchen. She seemed surprised to see him.

"You're up early," she said as she poured cream into her mug.

"I had a dream," he said as he took a seat at the small kitchen table. "Couldn't get back to sleep."

"Bad dream?" Mary asked. The boy could tell she was concerned, but she hid it well.

"I don't think so," he said. "Can't really remember. There was something there, and then it was just . . . gone."

"Dreams are like that. Don't read too much into them."

"I suppose," he replied. But he also suspected that this particular dream did mean something.

"Hot chocolate?" she asked.

"Yes," the boy said. "Thank you." He was pretty sure he liked hot chocolate.

Mary filled a small saucepan with milk, placed it on the stovetop, and turned on the gas. She sat down at the table across from him.

"I have something to show you," Mary said. She picked up her iPad, turned it on, and passed it across the table.

"This morning's *Post*," she said. "Look at the headline on the right side."

The boy took the iPad and glanced at the right-hand side of the page. Mary had not told him what he was looking for, but it immediately became evident.

The headline read: "Police Seek Identity of Mystery Boy."

He glanced up at Mary.

"Me?" he asked. "I'm the mystery boy?"

She nodded and took a sip of her coffee.

He tapped the headline with his index finger, and a new page quickly appeared. There — in full color — was the picture of him taken at the police station the previous night. He quickly scanned the article. It explained that he had been found at the National Gallery of Art and that he suffered from some form of amnesia. According to the article, the efforts to find his parents — or anyone who knew him — had so far proven fruitless. The police were seeking the public's assistance.

Mary stood up and tested the milk on the stove. She turned off the gas, poured the milk into a large cup, and stirred in a packet of hot chocolate mix. She placed the steaming mug in front of the boy.

"Not looking good, is it?" he said.

"It's still early," she said assuringly.

"Early for what?" The question came from the far side of the kitchen. It was Camille, dressed in dark blue pajamas covered with tiny images of the TARDIS — the time machine from *Doctor Who*. Her red hair flew off in all directions. She made her way over to the kitchen table and plopped down beside the boy.

"Morning, Art," she said. She glanced down at his image on the iPad. "Holy cow! Is that you? Mystery boy! How cool is that? You're a freakin' celebrity."

"Morning, Camille," he replied. "And I'm not a celebrity."

"Hot chocolate?" Mary asked Camille. Art appreciated Mary's effort to draw her daughter's attention away from the news article.

"Absolutely," said Camille. "And in my favorite mug?"

"Always," replied her mother.

Mary poured more hot milk into a large mug, stirred in hot chocolate mix, and handed the beverage to her daughter. Camille turned the mug so that the image on it faced Art. It was a painting of a har- bor, two boats loosely sketched in broad strokes on pale blue water. In the background was the sun — a small orange circle — its reflection rippling in the water below.

"Mom got this for me when she was in Paris," said Camille proudly. "It's my favorite. I'm going to Paris some-day, ya know. I want to see the Eiffel Tower, eat croissants, and wear a beret. That sounds very French, doesn't it? Mom says Paris is a great city."

Art stared at the mug.

"It's pretty, don't you think," said Mary as she sat down again at the breakfast table with her coffee. "And very famous. It's a painting by —"

"Claude Monet," said Art. His voice was calm. His eyes didn't leave the image on the mug.

Camille sat up straight in her chair. She could see the wheels turning in Art's head. Something was happening.

"Whoa," she said as she turned the mug back around in an effort to see if she had somehow missed Monet's name emblazoned upon it. Hot chocolate splashed on the table. "You know about the guy who painted this?" She was impressed.

"I know a lot about the guy who painted it," replied Art. "Claude Monet is one of the most famous painters in history. The painting's called *Impression, Sunrise.* The entire impressionist movement is named after that painting."

"The impression what?" asked Camille. Art sounded more like a teacher than a twelve-year-old.

"The impressionist movement," said her mother. "It was a style of art followed by a group of painters in the late nineteenth century. And he's right — the movement was named after the painting on your mug."

Mary turned to the boy. "So you know about the painting?" she asked. "Do you remember how you learned about it?"

The boy stared at the mug in silence.

"I know where I've seen that painting," he finally said.

"Good," said Mary. "In a book? Maybe a report you did at school?"

"No. I saw it in Paris."

6:43 a.m.
Saturday, December 16
National Mall, Washington, DC

Dorchek Palmer jogged eastward along the pea gravel path of the National Mall. To his right was the Castle, the original Smithsonian Institution—a beautiful Gothic structure of red sandstone. To his left was the imposing marble façade of the Smithsonian's Natural History Museum. Directly in front of him was the United States Capitol. It was still at least a half hour until sunrise, but the Capitol was, as always, brightly lit—a beacon at the end of the long grassy lawn that separated the majestic, ornate building from the simple marble obelisk at the far end. The Capitol Christmas Tree —a giant white spruce—stood between the reflecting pool and the Capitol.

There were only two more days before everything would be concluded. Yet, despite all their efforts, the spider—and the boy—remained hidden. Until the boy was found, the spider destroyed, and two more days had passed, the risk of failure still existed. Palmer thrived on risks, but he hated the feeling he might fail. He had to remain diligent. They would continue their pursuit. Perhaps the spider would stay in its hole, hidden from the world forever.

Perhaps.

But Palmer wasn't taking any chances.

He had scrubbed the laptop and the cell phone for any sign of the spider but had found nothing. His team would have to be more aggressive. There was no other choice.

Just as Palmer reached the end of the mall, a large black SUV pulled alongside the curb. Palmer glanced down at his watch. It was exactly 6:45 a.m. — the driver was on time. Palmer opened the back door and got in. A large cup of black coffee was in the cup holder and the morning's *Post* folded on the seat beside him.

Palmer took a sip of coffee as the driver pulled away from the curb. Palmer reached over, grabbed the morning paper, and casually turned to the front page. For one of the few times in his life, Dorchek Palmer was caught off-guard.

He quickly regained his composure. As bad as the situation appeared, there might still be some way to turn this to his advantage.

He pulled out his phone and called his team.

It was going to be an interesting morning.

CHAPTER 6

6:45 a.m.
Saturday, December 16
Sullivan residence, Washington, DC

"Paris?" exclaimed Camille. "You've been to Paris?"

Now she was really impressed.

"Maybe you saw it in a book," suggested Mary helpfully. Camille could tell by the tone in her mother's voice that she doubted whether Art had ever been to Paris. Her mother had been there once on business.

"I remember the museum," Art said. "It was sort of weird, like a house with lots and lots of paintings. And there was a park beside the museum. It was filled with all sorts of statues. We had lunch there—just some bread and cheese—on a bench. I think it was in the spring because there were flowers everywhere."

Camille looked at her mother for confirmation.

Mary nodded. "The painting's at a small museum in Paris that used to be a hunting lodge. It looks more like a house than a museum. And there's a park directly in front of the museum filled with statues."

"Wow," said Camille as she turned back to the boy. "So do you remember when . . ." Camille paused in midthought. She had almost completely overlooked something Art had said. "You said 'we' had lunch in the park. Someone was with you, right?"

The boy continued to stare at the mug.

"I can't see his face," he said.

"His face," Camille said. "Who?"

The boy shook his head. "I don't know," he said. "I can't see his face. I can't hear his voice."

Camille could hear the anxiety in the boy's words, and it worried her. She reached over and put her hands around the mug. The simple act seemed to break the spell. The boy looked away from the breakfast table. He seemed embarrassed.

"Sorry," he said. "I just thought that . . . well, I thought that it might be something."

"It *is* something," said Camille.

"Camille's right," Mary said. "It's a real memory — part of who you are. But there's no need to push too hard. The memories will come in time."

7:35 a.m.
Saturday, December 16
Starbucks, Washington, DC

Dorchek Palmer turned on his computer and pulled up the files he had secured from the laptop. There were twenty-three records in total — emails, documents, spreadsheets, presentations, photographs, and numerous other dossiers that would typically be found on anyone's computer. He had searched the laptop thoroughly, but there had been no sign of the spider.

Now Palmer was looking for something else in the files — something that might lead him to the spider.

Palmer clicked on the file labeled "Photos." A hundred or so thumbnails popped up — small images of buildings and people. He arranged the photographs by date and clicked on one of the most recent images. It was a picture of the Washington Monument.

Typical tourist, Palmer thought.

He clicked over to the next photograph. It was a picture of a blond-haired boy standing next to a tall blond-haired man, in front of the historical landmark.

Palmer clicked on the information icon at the bottom of the photo. A small window popped up with the timestamp for the picture.

December 12. 3:53 p.m.

Palmer retrieved the morning paper from a side table.

Bingo.

With the photograph in edit mode, he carefully cropped it and then saved the file to his desktop. He then forwarded a copy of the photo to each member of his team. Palmer sat back and took a sip of coffee. With any luck, they would have the spider by this afternoon.

CHAPTER 7

8:23 a.m.
Saturday, December 16
Sullivan residence, Washington, DC

"Grape or strawberry jelly?"

"Strawberry."

"Wrong. Grape's way better. Favorite movie?"

"*Star Wars*, I think." It was the first movie that popped into the boy's head.

"Yuck. Any of the Harry Potter movies is so much better. Favorite food?"

The boy sat at one end of the couch, Camille at the other. Camille's mother had decided that they would go to the National Gallery of Art at some point after lunch. She said it might help the boy remember. For the time being, however, he had to hang out with Camille while Mary finished up a couple of small projects for work.

The show *Adventure Time* played on the TV in the background, but Camille did not seem interested. She had questions—lots of them—and she was shooting them at Art in rapid fashion.

"I don't know," he replied. "Maybe spaghetti?"

"You're just saying that 'cause we had spaghetti last night," she said dismissively. "I think pizza's the best, but we only have it once a month. Mom says it's way fattening — but I know she likes it too."

"Pizza's good," the boy replied.

Camille rolled her eyes.

"Favorite animal?" she asked.

The boy paused for a moment. "I like dogs."

"Big dogs or little dogs?"

"Big, I suppose."

"Too messy," she said. "Cats are better. Have you been anywhere other than Paris — like London?"

He paused once more.

Good question. Had he ever been to London?

 An image immediately popped into the boy's head with startling clarity. Two men dressed in clothes from the Middle Ages standing by a table that was filled with all sorts of things — books, two globes, a sundial. And floating in front of the men was a weird white and black image — a hologram, almost, of a contorted and stretched skull. It was a painting — a painting the boy had once seen in London. It was called *The Ambassadors* by a man named Hans Holbein the Younger, and it was almost five hundred years old. The boy remembered being fascinated by the skull. Why, he wondered now, could he remember that he had seen this bizarre painting in London, but couldn't remember a single thing that really mattered about his life?

"Yes," he said. "I think I've been to London."

Camille shrugged. She was no longer impressed by his world travels.

"Ketchup or mustard?" she asked.

"Ketchup."

"Hmm, maybe. Favorite color?"

"Red."

"Apples or oranges?"

"Oranges."

"Wrong," she replied. "Apples are better 'cause—"

"Where's your dad?" the boy blurted out. He knew that the question was probably inappropriate, but it had just occurred to him that he had not seen any photos of Camille's dad—and no mention of him either. He knew that families did not always have two parents. He wondered about his own parents—his own family. Did he live with his parents? Maybe he lived with his grandparents, or an aunt or uncle. Did he have a brother or a sister? Did he come from a big family? He just didn't know. It suddenly, however, seemed important to know about Camille and her family.

"Don't know," said Camille nonchalantly. "I think he lives in California, but I've never met him."

"Never?"

"Never," replied Camille.

"That doesn't make you sad?"

"Why should it?" she said. "Mom said he didn't want kids. So it's just been me and Mom my whole life."

Camille did not seem the least bit upset about the situation with her father.

"Your mom's great."

It seemed like the right thing to say, and the boy meant it.

"Yeah," said Camille. "I just wish we could have pizza more than once a month."

She paused for a moment as if deep in thought. He worried that he may have overstepped his boundaries with the questions about her dad. Finally Camille looked at him. She had a serious expression on her face.

"Pool or beach?" she asked.

8:53 a.m.
Saturday, December 16
Chinatown Coffee Co., Washington, DC

Dorchek Palmer made his way through the front door of the narrow stone building while two members of his team assumed their positions outside the small coffee shop. He ordered an americano at the counter and then headed to a small table at the rear of the establishment. Taking a seat with his back to the wall, he placed his messenger bag on the floor next to him and waited. A little after nine o'clock, his appointment arrived. The man, perhaps thirty years older than Palmer, wore a tweed jacket and sported a large, unruly mustache. He ordered a cup of coffee and nervously made his way across the café, taking a seat at the table with Palmer.

"Well?" the man whispered. "Have you found it?"

"No," Palmer replied. "Soon."

"Soon?" said the man incredulously. "We need results now. Do you know what could happen if the wrong person gets their hands on it?"

Palmer nodded. "You'll have results," he said. "We've located the boy."

"You've found the boy?" the man said, a bit louder than intended. He caught himself immediately and lowered his voice. "Why didn't you say so? Problem solved, right? Surely the boy will get us what we want?"

Palmer reached into his messenger bag and retrieved the morning news. He opened the paper and spread it in front of him. "I take it you have not read the *Post* this morning?" he said beneath his breath.

The man sneered. "I only read the *Times* . . ." he started to say. And that's when he caught sight of the photograph on the front page of the *Washington Post*. Palmer glanced up at the man, who looked as if he'd taken a punch to the stomach.

"The police?" the man finally said. "The police have the boy? How could you let that happen?"

"The boy has amnesia," Palmer assured him, casually taking a sip of his americano. "He remembers nothing."

"But . . . but," the man sputtered, "what if he remembers? What if he's faking? What if he has . . . ?"

"We'll have the boy soon," Palmer said confidently. "The spider will follow."

"But your men lost him once," the man said.

"It was an unexpected turn of events," Palmer replied. "Just like the spider." He looked at the man over the rim of his coffee cup. It was clear Palmer had hit a nerve. Belette had been responsible for ensuring that any evidence of the spider had been destroyed. Had the man sitting across from him done his job as required, the spider would no longer exist.

"It is what it is," Palmer continued. "We deal with events as they exist, not as we wish them to be. I need you focused for this afternoon, not worried about what's already happened."

The man nodded. "I'll do my part."

"And I'll do mine," said Palmer.

The man paused. Palmer could tell there was something else the man wanted — needed — to ask.

"And what happens to the boy when you find him?" the man finally asked in a low voice.

Palmer carefully folded up the newspaper and took a final sip of his americano. Before he stood to depart, he reached down to pick up his messenger bag and looked the man directly in the eyes. "There are questions, Dr. Belette, that you should not ask."

CHAPTER 8

2:15 p.m.
Saturday, December 16
Sullivan residence, Washington, DC

There was a knock on the door.

"Leaving in five minutes," said Mary Sullivan. "Almost ready?"

"Almost," the boy replied. "Be there in a minute."

He stood in front of the floor-length mirror in the guest bedroom and looked at himself. Blond hair, green eyes. One ear seemed to sit a little lower than the other, but nothing so obvious that anyone would notice. He needed a haircut, or—then again—maybe he didn't. Maybe he liked his hair a little shaggy. There was nothing, he thought, particularly different or unusual about him. And while he recognized the face in the mirror, he couldn't attach a name, an address, a personality, or anything else to the person he saw looking back at him. No family. No history. Nothing.

And how did he know so much about Monet, or that painting in London? That didn't seem normal at all. In fact, it was downright weird that a twelve-year-old kid would know so much about stuff like that.

Shouldn't I be freaking out? he thought.

But he wasn't freaking out. And that worried him. And he could tell that it also worried Mary Sullivan, although she was doing her best to hide it from him.

He grabbed his jacket from the bed, pulled it on, and zipped up the front. It was time to go. He couldn't stare at himself in the mirror forever.

Mary and Camille were waiting at the front door. Camille was bundled up in a thick red ski jacket with white polka dots and a matching wool cap. The temperature had dropped below freezing overnight and still hovered just around thirty degrees. All the boy could think about was how much Camille looked like a giant strawberry.

"All set?" Mary asked. "Is the sweater warm enough? Do you want a thicker jacket? Camille might have something you could wear."

The boy shook his head. Mary had given him a thick sweater and washed the rest of his clothes. He was willing to put up with a little cold weather—he could only imagine what kind of jacket he might end up wearing if Mary pulled something out of Camille's closet. "I'm fine."

She offered him a pair of gloves—light blue with sparkles. "Camille's extra pair," she said apologetically.

"No thanks," the boy replied. He thrust his hands deep inside the pockets of his jacket. "I'll be okay."

Mary laughed. "I understand," she said with a wink. She handed him a knit cap. "You'll need this," she said. "It's a bit of a walk to the Metro station, but don't worry—the hat is sparkle free."

The boy pulled the cap down onto his head, then followed Camille and her mother out the front door, down the steps, and to the narrow brick sidewalk. It was cold outside, but the air felt refreshing on his face.

As he walked along the sidewalk, he felt objects in the pockets of his jacket. He pulled out three pennies, a wad of lint, and a paper clip from the left pocket. Deep in his right jacket pocket he found an old tissue and a small rectangular piece of black plastic. The piece of plastic had a small hole at the top and was engraved with white letters and numbers:

WB

WEST

28

He held the small collection of items from his pockets in his right hand as he walked.

"What's all that?" asked Camille, who was walking beside him. Her words formed little clouds of frost as she spoke.

"Just pocket junk," he said. He picked out the pennies and stuck them in his pants pocket. He looked around for a trash can to toss the rest of the bits and pieces away, but there wasn't one nearby. He stuffed it all back into a jacket pocket, figuring he could throw it away when he got to the museum.

2:17 p.m.
Saturday, December 16
First District Station, Metropolitan Police
Department, Washington, DC

"My mom's really embarrassed. This isn't the first time he's pulled this sort of stunt, but nothing as bad as this. Last year he just walked out of school after lunch one day and made his way over to the local movie theater. Nobody knew where he was, and everybody freaked out. We had teachers, my parents, neighbors, and the police looking for him all afternoon. Around five o'clock he called home and asked Mom to come pick him up. Claimed he had gotten food poisoning at school, passed out, and woke up in the theater. Can you imagine? Food poisoning. Nobody believed him, of course, but what could they say? Anyway, yesterday he told Mom that he was going to spend the night with one of his friends down the street—Jack Dudley. Mom called Jack's mom and made sure it was okay. School's out for Christmas, so Mom didn't care if he spent the night. Anyway, 'bout seven o'clock last night Mom called down to the Dudleys to check on him. Turns out he never showed up. Apparently he had called Mrs. Dudley and told her that he was sick and was going to stay home. Everybody freaked out again, but Mom didn't want to call the police because of what happened last time. We went to the movie theater, the mall, Dairy Queen—everywhere he liked to go. Spent all night looking for him."

The young man stopped speaking for a minute to take a sip of coffee. He wore a beat-up Baltimore Orioles baseball cap and thick black-rimmed glasses.

"So I'm driving around this morning," he continued, "looking for the little delinquent, when I get a text from one of my friends who had stayed in DC for the holidays—I go to school here at George Washington. He sends me a link to an article in the *Post* and asks if I recognize anyone. I almost ran off the road. There was Taylor—on the front page of the newspaper."

"Taylor?" asked Detective Neil Wasberger. "Your brother's name is Taylor, right?"

"Yes, sir. Taylor Patrick Howell. He's twelve years old, the youngest kid in our family. He lives in Winchester, Virginia, with my mom, my dad, and my middle brother."

"And you are David Howell?" Detective Wasberger furiously scribbled notes on his small notepad. Wasberger was a huge man—as wide as he was tall, and he was very tall. He stared down from his seat at the small, thin young man sitting in front of him. He had briefly considered calling Detective Evans to let her know that someone had shown up to claim the boy—to see if she wanted to come in and conduct the interview. But he had ultimately decided against it. It wasn't as if he were interrogating a criminal mastermind or something.

"Yes, sir," replied the young man. "My dad's out of the country on business, and Mom is real upset—especially since it's getting near Christmas. I told her I would come get him."

"And the name in the jacket?" The detective glanced at his notes. "It was Arthur, not Taylor."

David Howell laughed. "That's my middle brother —Arthur. With three boys, everything gets passed down. Sorta surprised he didn't have one with my name in it."

The detective nodded and made a notation in the file. The explanation made sense.

The young man leaned across the desk and handed a Virginia driver's license to the detective. "Here's my ID," he said. "Just in case you need to see it."

The detective looked at the license and handed it back. He then gave the young man a pen and pad of paper.

"I need your contact information," said the detective. "Address, home phone number, cell phone."

The young man jotted down the information and handed the pad back. The detective noticed a small tattoo on the inside of David's wrist. The young man caught Detective Wasberger staring at the tattoo and held up his wrist for the detective to see better. The tattoo was an image of a fleur-de-lis.

"Fraternity symbol," the young man said. "Kinda stupid, I suppose, but all the guys got one. My mom said it was trashy-looking."

"Listen to your mom," the detective said with a smile as he pulled back his sleeve to reveal a tattoo of Mickey Mouse riding a motorcycle on his forearm.

The young man laughed.

The detective glanced down at his notes. "I don't suppose you have any photos—"

"Of Taylor?" the young man interrupted. "Yes, sir. I'm sorry—I should have given you this earlier." He handed over a photo of the boy standing in front of the Washington Monument, next to a tall man with blond hair.

"That's my dad," David said. "He's a lawyer."

The detective placed the photo next to the photograph in the file. It matched perfectly. The boy was a mini version of his father, even if he didn't look a thing like his older brother. The mystery had been solved. Case closed. Detective Wasberger handed the photo back.

"Like I said, Mom's real embarrassed," said the young man.

"Tell your mom not to worry," replied the detective. "It happens more than you think."

The young man breathed a sigh of relief. "So it's okay if I go pick him up?" he asked. "I'd like to try to get him home before it gets dark. Mom's mad at him, but she's also worried sick."

"We can make that happen," said the detective. "I just need to get some paperwork filled out, put in a call to social services, and then set up a time for . . ."

David slumped back in his seat. The disappointment was evident on his face.

The detective paused. He knew that it would take forever to get in touch with social services and fill out all the necessary paperwork. And besides, he had robberies, homicides, and other real crimes to investigate. There was no sense in making this harder than it had to be.

The detective wrote down a name, address, and phone number on a piece of paper and slid it across the desk. "Your brother's in temporary foster care," he said. "That's the contact information for the foster parent. I'll give her a call and let her know you'll be picking up your brother."

The young man reached across the table, grabbed the detective's hand, and shook it vigorously. "I can't tell you how much this means to my family," he said. The detective could hear the emotion in the young man's voice.

"Just doing my job," replied Detective Wasberger.

"If you don't mind," David said, "do you know where in the museum my brother was found?"

The detective glanced down at his file. "According to the security report from the National Gallery, he was found in Gallery 83 on the main floor of the West Building. Doesn't mean a whole lot to me. Went through the museum once when I was on a high school field trip — never been back."

The young man shrugged. "Yeah," he replied, "guess it doesn't really matter."

The detective closed the file. "Do you want me to go with you to pick him up?" he asked. "You know, to put a scare in him for running away and lying about it?"

"Don't worry," David said. "I'll put a scare in him he'll never forget."

Dorchek Palmer made his way out of the police station. It was cold, and the day seemed to be turning colder by the minute. There was a security camera directly above the entrance to the station and a camera on each corner of the building. Palmer kept his cap pulled down low and tilted his head ever so slightly away from each camera he passed. He pulled out his phone and dialed it with his left hand. Palmer was right-handed, and it felt awkward using his left hand—but he knew that every detail mattered. Everything he did had to lead in a different direction—to a different person.

"Five minutes," he said into the phone before ending the call.

He then bent over and carefully tied his shoes—bright red Chuck Taylors. He positioned himself so that the cameras could get a good view of his feet.

Palmer checked his watch—a thick black sports watch. It was time to go.

He headed west until he ran into Sixth Street. He took

a right and headed north. A minute later a black SUV pulled alongside him. He opened the rear passenger-side door and quickly got in. A black trash bag sat on the seat beside him. He removed his hat, jacket, glasses, watch, and shoes and placed them into the bag. He pulled on a pair of well-worn leather loafers, a black wool jacket, black leather gloves, and a burnt orange skullcap.

"Wipe," Palmer said.

The man sitting in the front passenger seat tore open a small foil package and handed a wet wipe to Palmer. He cleaned the temporary tattoo off the inside of his wrist and dropped the dirty wipe into the trash bag. He then tied up the bag and handed it to the man in the front seat.

On the floorboard of the car was a black shoulder bag. Palmer retrieved an iPad from the bag and started punching in the information provided by the detective. Within minutes he had pictures of Mary Sullivan and her daughter and the address of their house sent to his team. A moment later he had retrieved her vehicle information and distributed that as well. He then pulled up the website for the National Gallery of Art and located an interactive map of the West Building. He located Gallery 83 — the gallery in which the boy had been found. Below the image of the map of the main floor — Gallery 83 highlighted in deep blue — were images of the significant works of art that could be found in that particular gallery.

Uh oh, Palmer thought.

It couldn't be a coincidence.

Palmer put the iPad away and stared out the window. The car turned down Seventeenth Street and moments later stopped in front of the World War II Memorial. Palmer grabbed the shoulder bag and exited the car, which immediately sped off. He started walking swiftly toward the Lincoln Memorial.

It had been only ten minutes since he had left the police station, but time was already running short.

CHAPTER 9

3:15 p.m.
Saturday, December 16
Archives Metro station, Washington, DC

Art, Mary, and Camille exited the escalator from the Metro station into a large plaza. A bitterly cold day greeted them —the temperature seemed to have dropped at least ten degrees in just the past half hour. In the middle of the plaza were two wide fountains. A freezing mist from the cascades blew across their faces. Small patches of dirty snow and ice hung tenaciously to the edges of the black stone that ringed each fountain. It seemed crazy to the boy that the fountain-heads would be operating in this weather.

On the sidewalk, a man sat on a crate playing a trumpet with one hand, his other hand tucked deep into the pocket of his thick winter coat. A small bucket for tips sat in front of him. The music seemed familiar to Art—slow and jazzy —but he couldn't remember the name of the song. The notes lingered in the cold air. Mary dropped a dollar into the bucket. The man paused ever so briefly to say thank you, then resumed playing.

Art looked up. Dark clouds hovered low in the sky, lending a dull gray color to everything he could see.

The boy and Camille followed Mary into the plaza and directly between the two fountains. A couple of tourists milled about, but the plaza was surprisingly empty and quiet.

"This is the Navy Memorial," said Camille. She pointed to a statue of a sailor on the far side of the plaza. "Pretty cool, huh? I call him Joe."

Art barely nodded. It was too cold for sightseeing.

Camille then turned and pointed to the massive stone building behind them. Engraved in stone—just above the center row of columns—were the words ARCHIVES OF THE UNITED STATES OF AMERICA.

"That's the National Archives," she said. "They keep the Declaration of Independence and the Constitution in there—the original ones, not copies. I bet it's full of all sorts of secret stuff. Mom said they even have stuff about UFOs."

Mary laughed. "That's true," she said. "I think Camille is planning to be a tour guide when she grows up. She knows all the little secrets about Washington, DC."

And she likes to talk, thought the boy.

"Well, as much as I enjoy Camille's travelogues," said Mary, "I think we need to get to the museum before our noses freeze off. Everybody wrapped up, tight and warm?"

"Toasty," Camille replied cheerfully.

"Yes, ma'am," Art said as he moved quickly alongside

Camille and her mother. They headed across the road and over to Seventh Street.

They turned down the avenue and into the full brunt of the cold December wind. The boy swore as he fell in behind Camille and her mother that his eyeballs were going to freeze. He pulled his knit cap down low on his head and squinted his eyes until he could barely make out Mary and Camille in front of him. Camille said something about how cold it had turned, but most of her words were lost in the wind. The boy just mumbled something and kept on walking.

After what felt like an eternity, Mary announced that they had arrived. Directly across the street was the National Gallery of Art—four stories high and spread across an entire city block. Long banners hung between the massive stone columns on the front of the building. The banners popped with color—brilliant greens, blues, and yellows. The image spread across the banners was a painting of a garden. The brush strokes in the print—blown up a hundred times or more their regular size—were enormous, bold ribbons of color. Across the top of the middle banner were the words "Lost Art: van Gogh Rediscovered."

The boy stared at the banners. They were beautiful.

"We're going to go see it," said Camille. "In February. We already have tickets."

"See it? See what?"

The girl pointed at the banners. "You don't know?" she asked incredulously. "It's a new painting by van Gogh."

"Not a new painting," corrected her mother. "A newly rediscovered painting. Everyone thought it was destroyed during World War II, but it was recently found in a bank vault in Germany along with a lot of other paintings. It's quite an exciting story."

"Well, it's a new painting to me," said Camille.

Mary ignored her daughter. "Anyway," she continued, "the National Gallery is purchasing the painting, and an exhibition has already been scheduled to begin in February. The crowds are going to be huge."

"One hundred and eighty-three million dollars!" exclaimed Camille. "They are paying one hundred and eighty-three million dollars for that painting. Can you imagine? I just have to see what a one-hundred-and-eighty-three-million-dollar painting looks like."

"What's the painting called?" asked the boy.

"*The Park at Arles with the Entrance Seen Through the Trees*," replied Mary. "Ever heard of it?"

The boy paused.

"I don't think so," he finally said. The truth, however, was somewhat more complicated. He remembered the way Mary had reacted when he recognized the painting on Camille's mug of hot chocolate that morning. It was as though she was waiting for him to freak out and run out of the room screaming. He didn't want to do that to her again. And yet, the truth was, he knew all about Arles—the small city in southern France, not the painting on the banners. And he also knew all about Vincent van Gogh—the brilliant and troubled Dutch painter. In fact, as soon as the boy had seen the words "van Gogh" on the banner, it was as if a faucet had been turned on in his head. The amount of information that had started gushing through his brain scared him. He knew that van Gogh was Dutch, that he had struggled as an artist, that during his lifetime he had sold only one painting, and that he had died penniless. But he also knew that van Gogh's paintings—raw, emotional, and filled with color—were brilliant beyond words. He knew that Vincent van Gogh had once lived in Arles and had produced some of his most mag-

 nificent works there—paintings bursting with color and energy. Van Gogh fed on the energy of the city, and it transformed how he saw the world around him—a simple still life of oranges became a dazzling display of dark blues, deep greens, and bright yellows. He knew that van Gogh had cut off his ear in Arles after an argument with another famous painter, Paul Gauguin. And he knew that van Gogh, whose life had ended far too young by his own hand, had almost died in that city.

But it was more than just trivia rushing through his brain. The boy was also positive that he had been to Arles. He could see the narrow stone streets, the red tile roofs, and the boats moored along the Rhône River. He knew there was a small café in Arles on the Place du Forum—the exact same café that van Gogh had painted so long ago. It was one of the boy's favorite paintings by van Gogh—the café brightly lit at night against a star-filled sky. The café and the surrounding street had changed little since van Gogh once lived in the city. Art could remember sitting in that café, sipping a Coke and realizing that Vincent van Gogh —one of the greatest artists in history—may have once sat in that same spot and looked out at the same street. The boy remembered the chill going down his spine at that thought.

And there was something else about Arles—a little itch at the back of Art's brain. He couldn't see it or name it, but the boy knew the detail, the story, whatever it was, was sitting there somewhere, waiting to be discovered. And that worried him.

3:16 p.m.
Saturday, December 16
First District Station, Metropolitan Police
Department, Washington, DC

Detective Neil Wasberger made a notation in the file that he had tried to call Mary Sullivan but had been forced to leave a message on her home phone.

She'll call back soon enough, he thought.

He was picking up the phone to contact social services when his somewhat sizable stomach growled rudely at him. He smoothed the front of his shirt, which was stretched tight across his belly, and thanked his lucky stars that he didn't have to wear a tie on the job—it was just one more thing that would grow a little tight around his build as time wore on.

Detective Wasberger checked his watch. It was well past his usual lunchtime—and the detective was not a man accustomed to missing lunch, or any meal, for that matter. His usual breakfast of pancakes, eggs, biscuits, bacon, and coffee barely sustained him through the morning on a normal day. He put the phone back down. He could call social services after a late lunch.

After all, what was the worst that could happen?

3:19 p.m.
Saturday, December 16
Sullivan residence, Washington, DC

The dingy gray delivery van pulled up in front of the narrow white-brick home near Dupont Circle. EDISON STREET COURIER SERVICE read the sign on the side of the van. A young lady wearing a dark blue jump suit and carrying a cardboard tube exited the van and made her way quickly to the front door. She rang the doorbell and waited a moment.

No answer.

She knocked twice on the door and waited another moment.

No answer.

She pulled out her phone and punched in a number. A moment later she could hear the phone inside the house start to ring. After five rings the answering machine picked up.

The house was empty.

The young lady returned to the van and, within seconds, pulled away from the curb. She made a right-hand turn down a narrow alley, which ran down the middle of the block behind the white-brick home. A short, thin man was waiting for her at the rear of the home. He climbed in the passenger side of the van.

"No one's home," said the young lady.

"Seems that way," said the man. "But her SUV is parked in back. They didn't go far." He pulled out his phone and sent a quick text message: "No one home, but car still here. What's next?"

The response was almost instantaneous: "Wait for my instructions."

3:22 p.m.
Saturday, December 16
Townhouse apartment, Washington, DC

Located on N Street between Seventeenth Street and Eighteenth Street in Washington, DC, are two rows of brick townhouses built in the late nineteenth century. The beautifully renovated town homes include two small hotels, an embassy, medical offices, and condominiums. One of the townhouses—a narrow four-story building painted a light gray—houses the American Society for the Preservation of Typewriters. At the rear of the building, four stories up and hidden from view, is a small, secluded apartment. For the past ten years, Dorchek Palmer has been its sole occupant. No one—not even the members of his team—knew about this apartment. Palmer always kept a hotel room downtown when he was in DC—it was where he would meet with his business partners, his clients, and his team. But the hotel was simply a cover. This small apartment off N Street was where his real work was done.

Palmer sat in front of a wall of flat-screen computer monitors and contemplated his next step.

He had hoped to find Mary Sullivan and the boy at home. The good news was that Sullivan, her daughter, and the boy were, in all likelihood, still somewhere in the city. His team would set up a perimeter and contact Palmer the moment the trio showed up. But that could be hours, and Palmer hated waiting. Fortunately, he was prepared for this type of situation.

Palmer opened up a tracking program he had developed the previous year and typed in Mary Sullivan's phone number. Within seconds the program had identified her cell phone carrier, her specific type of phone, and a list of every app she had on her phone. He scrolled through the list and tagged her camera app, her maps app, her emails, her social media accounts, and her text messages. His program would monitor her phone in real time and notify him the second she used any of those apps or functions. He would be able to identify where she was instantly.

Palmer checked his watch. It was almost time for Dr. Belette to play his part. Belette understood what was at stake, but that didn't give Palmer a lot of comfort. Belette was a nervous man, prone to stepping all over himself. Fortunately, Belette was also a greedy man, and Palmer believed that would make all the difference.

CHAPTER 10

3:42 p.m.
Saturday, December 16
West Building, National Gallery of Art,
Washington, DC

"Take my picture in front of it!" insisted Camille.

"Let's just get inside," said Mary Sullivan. "It's freezing."

Camille put her hands on her hips and stood on a small patch of brown grass just outside the National Gallery of Art. The huge banners hung directly behind her.

"Please take my picture," she said in a demanding yet polite manner.

Mary sighed. She knew it was easier just to take the picture than to continue to argue with her daughter. And to be fair, she also knew that she had a tendency to argue with her daughter for argument's sake—Camille had that kind of effect on people.

Camille motioned at the boy. "Get over here," she said.

The boy looked over at Mary, who merely shrugged. "I'd do what she says," said Mary.

The boy made his way over to Camille and stood next

to her. He realized for the first time how much taller he was than her—at least six inches, maybe more.

"Say cheese," said Mary.

"Elephant poop!" yelled back Camille.

The boy broke into a broad smile.

3:44 p.m.
Saturday, December 16
Townhouse apartment, Washington, DC

Dorchek Palmer's computer beeped. The Sullivan woman had used the camera app on her phone. The computer showed the image that was taken just seconds ago. There was no need to check the GPS tag on the picture—Palmer instantly recognized where she was.

It had to be a coincidence.

Palmer had plenty of questions, but those questions would have to wait—first things first. Palmer pulled out his phone and typed out a text message to his team. He stared at the message on the small screen of his smartphone. He knew that as soon as he sent the text, things were going to get a lot more complicated—but he had no choice. Palmer pushed Send.

The message read: "Package located. National Gallery of Art. West Building."

PART 2

"There is hidden in so many a heart a great and vigorous faith. We, too, are in need of this when we think of much that is in store for us."

—letter from Vincent van Gogh to his brother Theo,
30 May 1877

CHAPTER 11

3:55 p.m.
Saturday, December 16
East Building main conference room, National
Gallery of Art, Washington, DC

Andrew William Mellon was born in 1855 in Pittsburgh, Pennsylvania. Mellon made his great fortune—estimated in today's dollars at around forty billion dollars—as a banker, financier, and investor. He served as the secretary of the treasury to three presidents and as the ambassador to the United Kingdom. Mellon was a controversial political figure —President Franklin D. Roosevelt despised him. But notwithstanding all the accomplishments and controversy that defined much of his life, Mellon has ultimately become best known for the art he collected and a large stone building that now sits along Constitution Avenue between Fourth Street and Seventh Street in Washington, DC.

The West Building of the National Gallery of Art, designed by famed architect John Russell Pope in a neoclassic style, was Mellon's gift to the country he loved. But Mellon did not live long enough to walk the marble floors of the magnificent building—he died shortly after construction had started. And despite providing the funds for its creation and the artwork to be displayed, Mellon had insisted that the building should not bear his name. The grand building was completed in 1940 and dedicated in March 1941 by, of all people, President Roosevelt, the man who despised Mellon the most. The National Gallery of Art quickly became one of the grandest museums on the planet. Works by Rembrandt, da Vinci, Monet, Vermeer, Rubens, Raphael, and Whistler—to name but a few—quickly filled its walls. In 1978, an East Building—a structure of decidedly modern design connected to the West Building by a short underground concourse—was added to house the National Gallery's growing collection of contemporary art.

The National Gallery of Art is governed by a nine-member board of trustees that meets in a conference room in the East Building. Five of the trustees are appointed. They are men and women of the highest repute who have achieved great success in their chosen fields. Their ranks have included wealthy industrialists, Wall Street tycoons, philanthropists, educators, and Nobel laureates. The remaining four trustees are ex officio—that is, they serve as trustees because of the public offices they hold. The chief justice of the United States Supreme Court, the secretary of state, the secretary of the treasury, and the secretary of the Smithsonian Institution all serve as ex officio members of the board of trustees. Needless to say, a meeting of the board of trustees is no small matter. And that is exactly what had Kim Yoon so nervous.

Yoon had served as executive assistant to the National Gallery's deputy director for less than six months. Previously, she had worked at the National Gallery in various capacities while attending Georgetown University and had met celebrities, politicians, and wealthy socialites. She had grown accustomed to people with big egos and felt comfortable in almost any social setting. But nothing could have prepared her for one of her new duties as executive assistant: organizing a meeting of the board of trustees. She had to coordinate nine different schedules, security requirements (two of the trustees—the secretary of state and secretary of the treasury—stood fourth and fifth in the line of succession to the presidency of the United States), seating arrangements, the agenda, dietary demands, and numerous other miscellaneous details that had to be handled exactly right.

Yoon checked her list. The meeting was set to start at 4:00 p.m., and everything seemed to be moving along on schedule. Eight of the board members, the director of the National Gallery, and various administrative personnel milled around the room. The only board member who had yet to show up was the secretary of state. To be fair, Yoon had been warned. The secretary of state was a man known for his punctuality and precision—arriving exactly on time, demanding a strict adherence to a predetermined agenda, and concluding the meeting exactly on schedule. He was not, Yoon had been told, a man given over to frivolous and irrelevant discussion.

Yoon stepped into the hallway and glanced nervously at her watch. Three minutes to go.

She could hear the director inside the room calling the other board members to the large conference table. She could hear the shuffle of chairs as everyone settled into place.

Two minutes to go.

She glanced back inside the room. The board members —sans the secretary of state—had all taken their seats.

One minute to go.

A million thoughts rushed through Yoon's mind. Her heart pounded in her chest. Had she forgotten to confirm the meeting with, of all people, the United States secretary of state? Had he canceled at the last moment? Had she given his office the wrong time? The wrong date? What had gone wrong?

And that's when the door at the end of the hallway burst open and in strode the secretary of state of the United States of America. He was followed close behind by a small security detail and his assistant.

"Mr. Secretary," said Yoon. "My name is Kim—"

The secretary of state brushed past her without even acknowledging her presence, entered the conference room, and assumed his seat at the far end of the table.

"Let's get this meeting under way," said Damon Sacks, the United States secretary of state.

The time was exactly 4:00 p.m.

4:00 p.m.
Saturday, December 16
West Building, National Gallery of Art,
Washington, DC

Mary Sullivan, Camille, and Art made their way through a pair of massive bronze doors on the front of the museum, past the security desk, and over to the information booth, where they retrieved a map of the museum. Mary took a quick glance at the floor plan. "This way," she said as she headed toward a wide set of marble steps near the entrance.

Camille and the boy followed Mary up the winding staircase and into the rotunda of the National Gallery. The museum was filled with visitors, and the sounds of thousands of footsteps and whispered conversations echoed through the cavernous building. The rotunda, a large round room capped high above with a dome, was encircled with thick dark-marble columns. Between each column stood a tall Scotch pine adorned with simple white Christmas lights. In the center of the rotunda was a fountain, in the middle of which stood a bronze sculpture of Mercury, the Roman god of travelers and thieves. The fountain had been drained of water and filled with mounds of red poinsettias. Art looked up at the domed ceiling of the rotunda. Through the skylight in the center of the roof, he could see dark clouds outside. The clouds seemed to sit directly on top of the museum.

He turned to Mary. "So where do we start?" he asked. "Do we go to the room where they found me?"

Mary shook her head. "I think we should take it slow," she said. "Just treat this like a normal tour—give yourself a chance to get used to the museum. You ended up in that room, but there may be other reasons why you were in the museum. Let's walk around a bit and see if anything looks familiar."

The boy could tell she was nervous.

"See anything you recognize?" asked Camille.

The boy merely shrugged. "Don't think so," he replied. But that wasn't true. He recognized everything—the thick bronze doors that had greeted them as they entered the museum, the wide marble staircase, the rotunda and its circle of dark columns, and the image of Mercury pointing the way to some uncertain path. Why and how all of this was familiar to the boy remained lost to him.

He wondered if it had been a mistake coming back to the museum.

CHAPTER 12

4:05 p.m.
Saturday, December 16
East Building main conference room, National
Gallery of Art, Washington, DC

Damon Sacks was not a patient man, and he did not suffer fools gladly. And although he understood the need for the hastily called meeting of the board of trustees, it did not please him. At the far end of the room, the director of the museum, Elizabeth Downing, was excitedly discussing the details of the museum's latest planned acquisition —a long-lost painting by Vincent van Gogh, *The Park at Arles with the Entrance Seen Through the Trees.* The museum had agreed to purchase the painting for the sum of one hundred and eighty-three million dollars, a purchase made possible through a private charitable trust. And although the amount the museum was paying may have seemed outrageous, Sacks knew it was a wise investment.

The museum was so excited about the painting that it had already arranged a major exhibition to begin in less than two months. The exhibit, which had initially been scheduled to last for only a month, had already been extended into midsummer because of the huge public interest.

The story behind the painting was almost unbelievable. Long rumored to have been destroyed by fire during World War II, the painting—and reportedly several other lost works that had yet to be identified—had recently been found in a bank vault in Berlin. According to the art dealer who brokered the acquisition, the family who had owned the vault had barely escaped Germany with their lives at the outset of World War II and immigrated to the United States. The patriarch of the family—and the only member of the family who knew of the existence of the vault, where he stashed their valuable art collection before they left— died shortly after arriving in New York City. The family had settled into life in the United States, apparently under the belief that their amazing collection of artwork had either been captured by the Nazis or destroyed by fire. More than sixty years later, a representative from the German bank had appeared at the doorstep of the patriarch's grandson with some rather amazing news.

The family, although they had settled into a comfortable middle-class existence in their adopted country, had neither the desire nor the means to house and maintain the type of art collection left to them by their ancestor. Wishing to remain anonymous, they secured the services of a discreet art dealer from Switzerland to sell the collection. Their only request was that the United States—the country that had provided them safety from the Nazis—be provided the first opportunity to purchase the van Gogh painting, with promises of more paintings to come.

It was a unique opportunity for the National Gallery of Art. But Sacks also knew that buying a painting under these circumstances would not be easy—and not a matter to be taken lightly. The museum first had to comply with guidelines established by the American Alliance of Museums and the Association of Art Museum Directors to ensure that the painting had not been stolen by the Nazis during World War II. Paintings and other artwork identified as stolen by the Nazis would be returned to their rightful owners. The museum also had to establish the painting's provenance —that is, where it came from. The Van Gogh Museum in Amsterdam traced the painting's history from Theo van Gogh, Vincent's brother, to a family in Berlin in 1928. The paperwork provided by the bank and the art dealer filled in the rest of the story. The stringent museum guidelines had been more than satisfied.

The museum next had to establish the authenticity of the painting itself. Was it, in fact, a real van Gogh? Fake paintings abounded, and more than one museum had been fooled over the years. With a hundred and eighty-three million dollars on the line, Sacks did not intend to take anything for granted. He had insisted on the highest level of proof that the painting was authentic. And so the museum had retained the services of one of the world's foremost authorities to authenticate the painting. This man had been given unlimited access to the canvas; any resource or support he requested was provided to him. His only mission was to determine whether the painting was a real van Gogh, and the man's report was set to be delivered the following morning. Upon receipt of the summary, and assuming the painting was authentic, the transaction would likely be consummated and one hundred and eighty-three million dollars would be wired to an account in Switzerland.

"And now," said Director Downing, "I would like to introduce the man who has led the museum's effort to obtain the van Gogh—our director of acquisitions, Dr. Roger Belette."

4:07 p.m.
Saturday, December 16
West Building, National Gallery of Art,
Washington, DC

They made their way out of the rotunda and down the West Sculpture Hall. The boy knew they were heading in the opposite direction from the room in which he had been found. Camille talked the whole way, pointing to one sculpture after another. She had something to say about everything, but that was fine by him. Camille did a great job of keeping her mom occupied. Still, every now and then, the boy would catch Mary glancing over at him. He tried to keep his emotions off his face, but it was difficult— his heart was racing in his chest. He didn't recognize just some of the sculptures in the hall—he recognized them all.

They made their way into the maze of galleries that surrounded the West Sculpture Hall. The cold marble floors of the sculpture hall gave way to the wide oak planks of the galleries. The rooms were small, and the wood floors infused the galleries with a warm and intimate feel. The trio continued to make their way around and through the west wing—past the dark, moody retreats of Rembrandt van Rijn and the lively portraits of Frans Hals, into the formal elegance of Rubens, through a room filled with the colorful Madonnas of Raphael, and finally for a quick peek at a Botticelli or two.

"Anything?" asked Mary Sullivan as they reentered the rotunda.

"No," replied Art. He felt bad that he continued to lie to Mary. Everything was so familiar. He could have told her about any of the paintings that they had just walked past or the artists that had created them. He could have described how the painting *Girl with the Red Hat* by the Dutch master Johannes Vermeer showed his mastery of light, or how the elongated figures in the painting *Saint Martin and the Beggar* were a telltale sign of the painter El Greco. The boy felt completely at home in the museum, but he remained lost to himself. It was a strange feeling.

Mary bent down and looked Art in the eyes. "Are you up for the rest of our tour?" she asked.

"I want to keep going," he said.

Mary nodded. "Okay. But let me know if . . ."

"If I start to freak out?"

She smiled. "Yes. If you start to freak out."

"Anyone have eyes?" asked Dorchek Palmer.

The answers in his earpiece all came back negative, which was actually good news. Palmer sat in the Garden Café on the ground floor of the West Building of the National Gallery. He had lucked out, as the café was open later than usual due to a special holiday exhibit. Within minutes of ascertaining Mary Sullivan's location at the museum—and assuming his prey were going inside—he had dispatched his team, who had arrived straightaway to set up at each exit of the West Building, one member doubling up to keep an eye on the concourse leading to the East Building and one member remaining outside the structure. Three vehicles were parked within a block of the museum. Palmer knew that the West Building was far too big and had far too many rooms to conduct an effective ground search, particularly with only five team members and himself. So the first step was to secure the exits and identify the boy if he tried to leave. If they were lucky, the boy was still in the building.

Palmer had his iPad propped up in front of him at a corner table in the café. He had tapped into the museum's video security feeds—which were extensive—and was running the images in real time through sophisticated facial recognition software. If the software got a hit on the boy, his team would immediately move into action.

Palmer knew that there was no room for mistakes—the boy could not escape again. But Palmer had complete confidence in his team. What had occurred the last time was a fluke—the boy had been a surprise, and there had not been time for sufficient intel gathering and preparation. This time, however, his team was prepared. Palmer had hand-picked every member of his crew, recruited them all. They could break into the White House and steal the president's favorite pen, and no one would know. Catching a small boy would be no problem.

4:15 p.m.
Saturday, December 16
East Building main conference room, National
Gallery of Art, Washington, DC

"There is no question," said Dr. Belette, "as to the authenticity of this painting."

He pointed to an image of the van Gogh painting on the large video screen beside him on the wall. "Its provenance is well established. It has been subjected to every conceivable test and passed every one with flying colors. It has been examined by numerous experts on van Gogh, each of whom has unequivocally pronounced it as genuine."

"Not quite all of them," said a deep voice from the back of the room. "Dr. Hamilton has yet to render his final verdict."

The speaker was Damon Sacks, the secretary of state of the United States. Elizabeth Downing, the director of the museum, had feared that Sacks would interject himself into the process—he was known to push people's buttons simply to see how they responded. Downing knew that the only way to respond to Sacks was to push back when he pushed her—never back down. But would the bookish director of acquisitions have the internal fortitude to do that? Downing prepared herself to intervene. To her surprise, Dr. Belette seemed remarkably calm.

"A mere formality," Belette said confidently. "It is true that we still await Dr. Hamilton's final report, but I am confident that it will confirm what we already know."

"You are confident?" asked Sacks. "Dr. Hamilton was hired by this museum to be the final word on this painting. He is the leading authority in the world on art forgery. We are about to spend one hundred and eighty-three million dollars to purchase this painting. I need more than your confidence that the painting is authentic."

Sacks stood up, pushed his chair back, and glared across

the table at Dr. Belette. "I fully expected that Dr. Hamilton would be here today to address this board."

Uh-oh, thought Director Downing. She had received an email earlier that morning from Hamilton explaining that he was in the process of completing his report and would not be present for the meeting. The museum director started to stand in an effort to mediate. But Dr. Belette motioned for her to remain seated.

"Dr. Hamilton is the best there is," said Belette. "But his job — no disrespect — is not to put on a dog-and-pony show for this board — or you. His job is to complete his report so that this acquisition can be finalized."

Dr. Belette paused.

"I hesitate to speak further," he finally said, "for I fear he may have shared this with me in confidence." Belette's voice had dropped almost to a whisper. He spoke as if he were divulging a family secret. Everyone at the table — with the exception of Damon Sacks — leaned forward to catch his every word.

"When we spoke this morning," continued Belette, "Dr. Hamilton informed me that his report will absolutely confirm the authenticity of the painting."

The eyes of the board turned to Damon Sacks. The room was silent.

Sacks sat back down. He tapped his pen on the table.
Tick.

Tick.

Tick.

Tick.

"I'll await Dr. Hamilton's final report," he finally said—and the matter was concluded.

Elizabeth Downing—as well as everyone else in the room—breathed a sigh of relief. She glanced over at Roger Belette and nodded her approval.

Roger Belette took his seat at the table as Elizabeth Downing brought the meeting to a close. His head felt as if it would explode. He had feared that he wouldn't make it through the meeting and the inevitable resistance from the board's notoriously acrimonious member. But Belette had. And in the aftermath of his confrontation with the secretary of state, the board had voted unanimously to approve the acquisition of the van Gogh painting as soon as Dr. Hamilton's final report was received—assuming, of course, that it confirmed that the painting was authentic. But Belette had every confidence that Hamilton's report would absolutely, and without any question, corroborate that fact. Belette, after all, had written that report, which would be delivered via email to Elizabeth Downing at precisely nine o'clock the following morning.

CHAPTER 13

4:35 p.m.
Saturday, December 16
West Building, National Gallery of Art,
Washington, DC

There was no longer any pretense that this was a normal visit to the museum. The boy and the Sullivans made their way out of the rotunda again and quickly down the East Sculpture Hall, past the tall marble sculptures and enormous urns. Camille offered none of her usual running commentary. They passed through a small gallery of paintings of Native Americans and into a large garden courtyard filled with plants.

The boy pointed to an open passageway on the left side of the courtyard. "Over there," he said. His pace quickened. He was now walking several steps ahead of Camille and her mother.

Camille started to speed up to catch him, but her mother grabbed her by the arm. "Give him some space," she said.

Camille slowed down without a word of protest and walked at her mother's side.

The boy disappeared into the open passageway. Moments later, Camille and her mother arrived and stepped into the gallery. Paintings by Edgar Degas and Mary Cassatt lined the walls.

"We're close," Mary whispered to her daughter.

"But where's Art?" Camille asked.

Mary pointed to an opening to their left.

They made their way across the room and stood at the threshold leading into the next gallery. A small sign affixed to the interior of the doorway pointed into the area beyond. The sign read GALLERY 83.

The boy stood on the far side of the room. In the middle of the space was a relatively small sculpture—barely more than three feet in height—of a young ballerina. It was entitled *Little Dancer Aged Fourteen* by Edgar Degas. A wide bench sat directly in front of the sculpture.

"Is this . . . ?" asked Camille as they slowly approached the sculpture.

"Yes," replied her mother. She pointed to the bench. "That's where he must have been sitting when they found him."

"That's funny," said Camille.

"What's funny?"

"He's not staring at the sculpture now," the girl said.

Mary Sullivan looked at the boy. Her daughter was right. The boy wasn't staring at the sculpture. Instead, he appeared to be intently studying the paintings on the wall

—bright, colorful portraits and paintings of landscapes, flowers, and fruit.

"The paintings," said Camille. "Who painted them?"

"Vincent van Gogh," replied her mother. "And a painter named Paul Gauguin."

Mary turned and looked at the wall behind her. The room was filled with paintings by van Gogh and Gauguin. It occurred to her that when the boy was found, perhaps he had not been staring at the sculpture by Degas—maybe he had been staring at the paintings.

And from the expression on the boy's face, it seemed that he had come to the same realization.

He walked from painting to painting.

He stood in front of a self-portrait of Vincent van Gogh painted in 1889—the artist, staring intensely at the viewer, hold-ing a palette and brushes, his red hair and beard in striking contrast to the brilliant blue background that seemed to fold the world in around him. It was a portrait of a tortured soul and deep introspection. Van Gogh, Art knew, had spent most of his short life desperately searching for himself and for his place in the world.

A self-portrait of Paul Gauguin hung just a few feet away. Painted the same year as van Gogh's self-portrait, it was a sharp contrast to the startling intensity of the van Gogh. Although the colors were every bit as bright—brilliant yellows, greens, and reds infused Gauguin's painting—the paintings could not have been more different. In his self-portrait, Gauguin does not meet the viewer's gaze—rather, he looks confidently beyond the viewer to the broader world.

As the boy turned around and examined the room, he understood that the other paintings in the gallery revealed that same contrast—van Gogh's efforts to capture, define, and understand the small, narrow world in which he lived, and Gauguin's ever-expanding view of that same world.

But despite the differences that separated van Gogh and Gauguin—and there were many—the boy knew of one fact that had brought these men together at a specific time and place. For nine weeks in 1888, Vincent van Gogh and Paul Gauguin had lived together in a small village in southern France—Arles. Now they appeared to be sharing space again, this time in Gallery 83.

Beep.

Dorchek Palmer glanced down at his iPad. The facial recognition software had found a match. He checked the location—Gallery 83. Palmer knew this was in the east wing of the West Building.

Great, he thought, just freakin' great.

He pulled up the video feed on his iPad. The gallery was crowded, and it took a moment for him to locate the boy. Finally Palmer found him standing on the far side of the room, staring at a self-portrait by Vincent van Gogh.

Oh, for the love of . . .

Palmer pulled out his floor plan of the museum. He had two team members relatively close to the gallery: one was stationed just down the East Sculpture Hall and through the rotunda, at the main entrance next to the National Mall; and another, Regina Cash, was waiting at the east entrance, which was a floor below the gallery in which the boy was now located. Palmer needed eyes on the boy immediately —as good as the video cameras may have been, they didn't cover everything, and it was easy to lose someone in a crowd.

He decided to go with Regina Cash, in order to keep the other team member at the main entrance. He sent her a quick text: "Gallery 83, east wing, main floor. Locate boy and follow. Do not intercept."

A moment later Palmer received a return text: "On my way."

CHAPTER 14

4:45 p.m.
Saturday, December 16
West Building, National Gallery of Art,
Washington, DC

Camille watched as the boy slowly made his way around the gallery. He moved in a counterclockwise direction and paused at each painting. Carefully studying each work of art, he repositioned himself occasionally to examine a small detail or to look back at paintings he had already scrutinized as if in comparison. When the boy finally came full circle and arrived back at the doorway they had used to enter the gallery, he silently took his place beside the girl. Camille said nothing. She understood that it was not the time for words.

They stood there in silence and simply watched the flow of patrons through and around the room.

"How about a snack?" Mary Sullivan asked finally. "The café downstairs is nice."

The boy nodded, and the three visitors departed the gallery without another word.

Regina Cash made her way to the main floor and stationed herself along the East Sculpture Hall. She spied the boy almost immediately. He was accompanied by the Sullivan woman and her daughter—Cash recognized them from the pictures Palmer had sent her earlier that day. Cash nonchalantly moved to the side of the hall and pretended to look at a sculpture.

"Got him," she said in a whisper. "Heading toward the rotunda."

Her words were instantly transmitted to the small receiver in the ear of each team member.

Cash made a quick turn as soon as the boy passed and fell in with the rest of the tourists trailing behind him. When they reached the rotunda, the boy, Mary Sullivan, and her daughter turned right and headed for the stairs leading to the ground floor. Cash fell a few feet back but stayed close enough to maintain visual contact.

"Constitution Avenue," she whispered. "Tag. You're it."

Eric McClain was the team member assigned to the exit leading to Constitution Avenue. He moved into position as soon as he heard the transmission from Regina Cash. A moment later he saw the boy and his entourage exit from the stairwell.

"Tagged," he whispered.

The plan was to intercept them as soon as they left the

museum and separate the boy from the woman and her daughter. The roper was already waiting, and McClain needed to confirm which exit they would use. Timing, he knew, was crucial. But the trio didn't head for the exit. Instead, upon reaching the small foyer at the bottom of the stairs, they turned toward the center of the museum. McClain followed close behind.

"Still in the house," he said into his transmitter.

McClain stayed close behind as the small group made their way over to the Garden Café, directly in the middle of the ground floor. He watched as they spoke briefly to the hostess, who then escorted them across the café to a small table near a fountain.

"Garden Café," McClain whispered. "Tag. You're it."

He glanced over at Dorchek Palmer, who sat in the café less than ten feet from the boy. McClain nodded ever so slightly in Palmer's direction, turned, and departed.

CHAPTER 15

5:05 p.m.
Saturday, December 16
West Building, National Gallery of Art,
Washington, DC

Nothing.

Although his head was filled with all sorts of facts and information about the museum and the artwork inside it, the boy still knew absolutely nothing about himself. He had cautiously hoped that it would all come rushing back to him as soon as he had stepped into the museum, or saw the right painting, or sculpture, or whatever it was that had brought him to the museum in the first place. He had hoped that all the memories of who he was and why he had been found here would be waiting for him. He had hoped to find himself in the museum, but the boy remained lost.

Part of him wondered if the memories had ever existed. Maybe Art had always been some sort of blank slate. He knew it sounded absolutely ridiculous, but that's how he felt —empty and unformed. He had no awareness of himself as anything other than what he was right now. No history. No family. No memories. Nothing. Just a boy who seemed to know way more about art than any twelve-year-old should know, sitting in the middle of one of the most famous museums in the world, with no idea why he was here.

"You okay?" Mary Sullivan asked. "You've barely touched your pie."

"I'm okay," the boy said. "I was just . . . expecting, you know, something."

"I know." Mary pointed at his head. "You're in there somewhere. The memories will come when you're ready."

The boy nodded. He had heard that before.

But what if the memories never returned?

Mary glanced down at her watch. "The museum is closing, and we need to be heading back home soon," she said. "Snow's supposed to come down hard tonight, and I don't want to get caught in it. I'm going to run to the ladies' room before we get going. Will you be okay while I'm gone?"

Camille looked up from her chocolate cake, half of which appeared to be smeared across her left cheek. "You have to be kidding," she said. "We're not a couple of little kids."

"Fine!" said Mary in mock exasperation. "Forget I even asked. Now, may I run to the ladies' room before I pull a Tycho Brahe?"

Camille burst out laughing. "Yes, ma'am," she said. "And watch out for drunk moose!"

The boy looked at Camille. "Tycho what? Drunk moose?"

Camille turned to her mother. "See," she said triumphantly, "he doesn't know everything."

Mary rolled her eyes. "Fine," she said. "Then feel free to
bring him up to date on sixteenth-century Danish astrono-
mers and their weird pets. I'll be right back."

Mary gathered her purse and headed toward the restroom on the far side of the café.

Camille wasted no time.

"You see," she said, "Tycho Brahe was an astronomer a
long, long time ago, and he had this pet moose . . ."

The boy listened patiently as Camille explained—in
her own unique, rambling manner—about Tycho Brahe the
Danish astronomer and his pet moose, and how Brahe had
died when his bladder exploded, which Camille thought
was an incredibly gross way to die. She then started to discuss what a bad pet a moose would make.

But the boy was no longer paying attention to Camille.
Something else suddenly had his attention: an old woman
sitting at the table behind Camille had just pulled a small
black piece of plastic from her purse and placed it on her
table. Art immediately reached into his coat pocket and dug
around until his fingers settled on the object he was looking for. He pulled it out. It was the black rectangular piece
of plastic he had found in his jacket earlier that afternoon.
It was identical to the piece of plastic sitting on the table
behind Camille.

"Hey," said Camille, who had finally noticed that the boy was no longer paying attention to her. "I'm talking, here —little education for you."

Art motioned for her to be quiet. "Shhh," he said. He wondered, should he just ask the woman what the little piece of plastic was?

Camille leaned across the table. "What's going on?" she asked. "Did you remember something?"

The boy shook his head. "No," he said. "I'm just trying to . . ."

His words trailed off as he tried to decide what to do.

Just ask her, he told himself.

But before he could act, a gray-haired man in a bright yellow sweater approached the woman. They appeared to be about the same age—perhaps it was her husband.

The woman handed the older man the piece of plastic. "Get our jackets," she instructed, "and I'll meet you up by the exit. I need to go by the gift shop. I promised Sal I would pick something up for the kids."

The husband took the small piece of plastic, shrugged, and, without a word, started shuffling across the café toward the exit. The boy stood to follow, but Camille immediately grabbed him by the arm.

"Where are you going?" she asked. "We're supposed to wait here."

The boy held up the rectangular piece of plastic for Camille to see, as if that clarified everything.

"I have to . . ." he started to explain. Camille stared at him as if he were crazy, but what more could he say?

Maybe I am crazy, he thought.

He pulled his arm free from Camille and hurried to catch up with the man in the yellow sweater.

Camille stared at the boy as he quickly made his way across the café. She knew that if he went into the hallway and back into the main part of the museum, she would lose him completely.

Mom told me to watch out for him. And I promised I would.

She glanced in the direction of the restrooms, but there was no sign of her mother, and Camille had no means of letting Mary know what was going on. Despite months of pleading, Camille had still not convinced her mother to get her a cell phone, even though every other kid in her class had the latest iPhone or Android. Her mother could be very old-fashioned sometimes.

Camille knew she had no choice. She sprinted across the café to catch up with Art.

When the Sullivan woman had gotten up and headed for the restroom, Palmer had a feeling that the three of them would be leaving the museum soon. He had alerted his team to be ready. He was caught off-guard, however, when the boy got up and left the table in a rush, immediately followed by the girl. Palmer had been pretending to read his iPad while stealing occasional glances at the boy so he wasn't sure what prompted the hasty departure. He glanced over at the women's restroom, but the girl's mother was nowhere to be seen. It wasn't exactly how Palmer had planned it, but the team had to act.

"Heading toward the west entrance," Palmer said.

"West entrance in place," responded a voice in his ear.

"Roper's on the way," another voice said.

Palmer pulled up the video feed for the west entrance on his iPad and settled back to watch.

CHAPTER 16

The boy followed the older gentleman down a short hallway, through two large rooms lined with antique furniture,
and into a wide gallery filled with modern art. The man
passed quickly through this room and up a short set of
stairs. Art was amazed at how quickly the man was moving. However, just as the man reached the top of the stairway and was about to enter the next room, he paused to
catch his breath. The sudden change of pace caught Art
off-guard, and he stumbled as he stopped short of the
stairway—his sneakers squeaking loudly on the polished
marble floor. The older man glanced back over his shoulder at the unexpected sound. Art turned his head just in
time to avoid direct eye contact and pretended that he was
staring at a large bronze sculpture of a woman and a deer
that stood in the middle of the hallway. By the time Art
had turned back around, the old man had resumed walking

and was headed toward the far corner of the next room. A moment later, he was out of view.

Art cautiously began mounting the stairs and peeked over the top of the steps into the next room. He could see a wide desk, a pair of security guards, and a set of large bronze doors leading to the outside. He moved to the top of the stairs, paused for a moment, and then entered the space. The older gentleman was nowhere to be found.

Art's heart started beating furiously.

How could he have lost him?

Where did the old man go?

Art felt himself starting to panic. The small piece of plastic that he held tightly in his right hand might have been the first real clue to who he was — and he had just blown it.

Calm down, the boy told himself. The old man didn't simply disappear into thin air.

Art took a deep breath. The pounding in his chest started to slow down. His thoughts became clearer. He noticed an open passageway on the far left side of the room.

That must be where he went.

The boy headed across the room toward the corridor, glancing over at the security guards near the entrance as he walked. One of the guards caught his eye and nodded at him. The boy nodded back, acting as if he knew exactly where he was heading and why. He reached the passageway and glanced inside. The older man stood at the end of a short hallway in front of a long counter made of gray granite. There was a black sign with white lettering above the man's head:

WEST BUILDING
WEST ENTRANCE CHECKROOM

Art could see racks filled with coats behind the counter. A moment later, a young lady appeared on the opposite side and handed the older gentleman two large winter coats. He thanked her, turned around to leave, and almost ran headlong into Art.

"Sorry," said Art.

The old man mumbled something and moved past the boy toward the exit.

Art looked down at the small chip of plastic in his hand. A piece of the puzzle fell into place.

Camille was almost out of breath by the time she caught up with Art. She found him standing near an exit and staring down a short hallway.

"What are you doing?" she demanded. "Mom's going to be so mad."

Art pointed to the counter at the far end of the corridor and to the lady standing behind it. He held up the small plastic object for Camille to see.

"WB," he said. "It means West Building, which is where we are. And 'west' means the west entrance."

"So?" said Camille.

"Don't you get it?" the boy said. "It's a checkroom—people leave all sorts of stuff here that they don't want to carry around the museum—coats, umbrellas, bags, those kinds of things. They give these little plastic chips to people when they leave something."

"You think you left something here?" Camille asked. But Art didn't respond—he was already making his way over to the checkroom counter. Camille glanced around for any sign of her mother. Nothing.

Camille briefly considered heading back to the café. She knew her mom would freak when she discovered they were missing. But Camille had promised her mom that she would keep an eye on Art. She turned and followed him down the short passageway.

"They're at the west entrance checkroom," said Palmer.

"I have visual," said a voice in his ear.

"Roper ready?" asked Palmer.

"Fifteen seconds," replied another voice.

"Don't mess this up," said Palmer.

No one responded. They all understood the consequences.

Camille hustled to catch up with her wayward charge at the checkroom counter.

"May I help you?" the young lady behind the counter was asking Art.

Art handed her his small plastic chip. The lady smiled politely, took the chip, and read the small number printed on it.

"Just a second," she said as she disappeared into the back of the checkroom.

The boy pointed to the checkroom sign. "Five minutes ago I had no idea what that plastic chip was."

He paused.

"I left something here," he finally said, to Camille or perhaps to himself.

Any concerns Camille may have had about her mother vanished.

"A clue," she said. "About you."

The boy nodded. "Yes," he said. "A clue about me."

Mary Sullivan made it to the middle of the café before she realized something was wrong—there was no sign of Camille or Art at the small table at which she had left them just a few minutes prior. She stopped for a moment and surveyed her surroundings. The café was located in the middle of the ground floor of the West Building. To her left and right were long hallways leading to the west and east entrances to the museum. Directly in front of her was the entrance onto Constitution Avenue.

Calm down, Mary told herself.

Perhaps she was simply confused.

Perhaps she was looking at the wrong table.

She took a deep breath and carefully examined the small café once more.

She quickly realized, however, that she had been looking at the right table. She could see Camille's empty plate and Art's barely touched piece of pie.

Mary tried to push the simmering sense of panic to the back of her mind, but it was difficult. Did this have something to do with the boy? He had simply appeared at the museum the day before—no name, no memory. Mary wanted to kick herself. Why had she thought it was a good idea to bring him back here? Why had she left the kids alone for even a minute?

She looked around for Camille's bright red explosion of hair. It was always the best way to find her in a crowd.

But there was nothing. No red hair. No red jacket with white polka dots. No Camille. No Art.

Mary stepped to the hallway to her left. It led to more

galleries and to the west entrance. There was no sign of her daughter.

She moved quickly back across the café to another long hallway—this one leading to the gallery shop and east entrance. Nothing.

Mary's heart beat furiously in her chest. It took everything in her power to keep from screaming out Camille's name.

She made her way over to the small foyer just inside the exit to Constitution Avenue. Nothing. She looked around the foyer as if Camille and the boy might be hiding in a corner somewhere.

A security guard standing near the entrance approached her.

"Are you okay? The museum is closing, and we're asking everyone to leave," he said.

Mary realized that she must have looked frantic—standing in the foyer and turning in circles.

"I . . . m-my daughter . . ." she stammered. "I can't find her."

"It's okay," the security guard assured her. "We're here to help. Everything will be fine."

But Mary Sullivan was not convinced that everything would be fine.

CHAPTER 17

5:45 p.m.
Saturday, December 16
West Building, National Gallery of Art,
Washington, DC

The girl in the checkroom seemed to be taking forever. She had disappeared into the recesses of the backroom for more than a minute and had yet to reappear.

Art leaned over the counter and tried to see what she was doing.

"Maybe you didn't leave anything," suggested Camille. "Maybe you just found that plastic thing on the floor."

Art shook his head. "No," he said.

There was a shuffling noise from the back of the checkroom.

"Found it," they heard the girl call.

She appeared a moment later carrying a small brown backpack. She double-checked the number on the plastic chip against the paper tag tied to the backpack.

"Here you go," she said as she handed over the backpack to Art. "Sorry it took so long."

The boy took the bag and immediately headed back toward the entrance foyer.

"Thank you," Camille said to the cloakroom attendant before she turned to follow Art. "He's a little excited."

Camille found the boy sitting on a marble bench in the large foyer. He was looking at the back of the backpack. She took a seat beside him.

"My name's Art," he said.

"I know," Camille replied. "I liked that better than Arthur."

"No," he said. "It really is Art. Look." He pointed to a white label on the back of the backpack. It had a place to fill in a name, phone number, and address. Only the name was filled in. "Art H.," it read in black magic marker.

"Wow," said Camille. "So your last name begins with an *H*. Do you know what the *H* stands for?"

The boy shook his head. "Not yet," he said. He turned to Camille and smiled. "But we're finally getting somewhere. Things are definitely getting better."

"Can you describe your daughter for me?" asked Dexter Poss.

Poss had served as a security guard for more than ten years at the National Gallery of Art. In that time, he had seen hundreds of parents just like the lady standing in front of him—panicked and emotional. He always tried to assure them that everything was fine—the children were inevitably found, usually much calmer than the parents looking for them.

"Ten years old," replied the lady. "Bright red hair—you can't miss her. Her name's Camille. Camille Sullivan. I'm her mother, Mary."

Poss scribbled down the information as Mary spoke.

"And the boy?" he asked.

"Blond," she replied. "A couple years older than my daughter and much taller. He's wearing a blue jacket."

"Don't worry," the security guard assured her. "We have a standard procedure in these situations. It's very effective —we haven't lost a child yet. We'll track them down in no time."

Poss was just about to suggest that Mary return to the café—in case the kids showed up looking for her—when they were interrupted by a short middle-aged lady wearing thick glasses.

"Excuse me," the woman said, "I couldn't help but over-hear you say that you're looking for a young girl with red hair?"

"Yes!" said Mary excitedly. "Have you seen her?"

"Was she wearing a bright red jacket?" asked the lady. "White polka dots?"

"That's her!" exclaimed Mary. "Where?"

"Ground floor gift shop," the lady said as she pointed toward the center of the museum. "Back right corner near the children's section—not more than a minute or so ago. She really stands out."

Dexter Poss smiled. Case closed.

Regina Cash watched as the security guard and Mary Sullivan hurried toward the gift shop. Cash had just bought the roper a little more time. Now she needed to disappear before the security guard and Sullivan returned, having found no kids. Cash pulled on her jacket and headed out into the cold winter day.

CHAPTER 18

5:52 p.m.
Saturday, December 16
West Building, National Gallery of Art,
Washington, DC

"So?" asked Camille. "Are you going to open it?"

The question caught the boy off-guard.

"Yeah, I guess so," he said.

He had been so excited to discover that his name really was Art that he had forgotten to open the backpack and actually see what was inside. He had noticed, however, that the bag did not seem particularly heavy.

"Well, what are you waiting for?" Camille said. "Open it."

Art examined the backpack, which appeared perfectly normal if a bit ragged around the edges. He unzipped the top, reached in, and pulled out a baseball cap—a well-worn, sweat-stained dark blue baseball cap with the initials NY on the front.

Camille looked at him. "A Yankees fan?" she said. "Seriously?"

The boy shrugged his shoulders. "I guess," he said. But

as soon as he had seen the cap, he'd known. He was a Yankees fan. He put the cap on his head. It fit perfectly—the kind of fit a person gets only after a hat has been worn a thousand times.

The boy reached into the backpack again and pulled out a can of Coke.

"I prefer Coke Zero," said Camille. "All the flavor and none of the sugar."

Art wondered if she would be offering a running commentary throughout this entire exercise.

Next was a set of black winter gloves, which he placed on the bench. The gloves did not have the slightest hint of sparkles—a good thing.

"Anything else?" Camille asked.

Art opened the pack wide. "Nothing," he said. The disappointment was obvious in his voice.

"Check the front pocket," she said. "I always throw all sorts of junk into the front pocket of my backpack."

Art opened the front pouch and turned the backpack upside down. The contents of the pocket spilled out onto the bench.

"Holy cow!" Camille exclaimed. Sitting on top of the pile of stuff that had fallen from the backpack was a small wad of bills. Camille picked up the bills and counted them.

"This is more than four hundred dollars," she said. "You're friggin' rich."

"I'm not rich," replied Art. Then again, it occurred to

him, he might be. It wasn't as if he actually remembered if he was rich or not.

"What else is there?" he asked in an attempt to distract Camille from her obsession with the money.

"A pencil," she said. "Worthless." She pushed it to the side.

She held up a small crumpled piece of paper, which she then folded flat on the bench. "A receipt," she said, looking closely to read it. "From some coffeehouse. Worthless."

She turned back to the pile and sorted out several tissues, some coins, a rubber band, a couple of empty candy wrappers, and a stick of gum still wrapped in its shiny silver foil. Only two items remained — a brass key and a small piece of white plastic, about the size of a credit card.

Camille held up the key. The bow — the round part that is used to turn the key — was painted a deep blue with the number 10 engraved in black. "Ring any bells?" she asked.

Art took the key and carefully examined it. "No. Nothing."

He handed the key back to Camille — she had become the curator of the backpack junk. She dropped the key back into the pile.

Art picked up the piece of white plastic and turned it over in his hand.

"Look," he said. On the reverse side of the plastic was a series of numbers: 01284267931248.

"What is that?" Camille asked.

"No idea," the boy replied. "Maybe your mom will

know." He stuck the white plastic card back in the pile with the rest of the stuff that had fallen out of the front pocket.

"Is that it?" asked Camille. "Nothing else?" The disappointment was now evident in her voice.

"I think so," Art said. He picked up the backpack and examined it. The front pocket was empty, as was the main part of the backpack. He shook the backpack just to make sure. As he did, something shifted around inside the bag.

"Did you hear that?" asked Camille. "There's something still in there."

Camille was right—something else was in the pack. But where?

Art ran his hand deep inside the bag and felt around.

Nothing. The backpack appeared to be completely empty.

The boy shook the bag again. Something was definitely shifting around inside.

Art ran his hand down inside the pack once more. This time he found a loose seam—the interior lining of the backpack had separated from the padded back of the bag. Art put his hand inside the lining. He felt something smooth and pulled it out. It was a small leather journal.

The cover of the journal was dark brown, dry and cracking along the spine and covered with scuff marks and scratches. Art opened it and thumbed through the pages, which were yellowed with age and covered with fine cursive script and small drawings. One of the pages was tabbed with a small yellow Post-it note—clearly a recent addition. Art opened the journal to that page.

On the top half of the page were two small drawings, both contained within rectangles. On the left was a drawing of a young girl holding some sort of basket in her lap. The girl wore a scarf around her head and stared directly out at the viewer with dark eyes. Beneath the image of the girl was the word "recto." To the right of the image of the young girl was another rectangle—identical in size and shape to the one on the left—with the word "verso" directly beneath it. This rectangle was blank with one exception—in the upper right-hand corner was a strange, almost abstract shape. It looked as if someone had dropped a bit of ink on the page and it had splattered in all directions.

Camille pointed to the words beneath the drawings —the same fine cursive handwriting as the rest of the journal.

Alfred Guillou

Une Jeune Fille Avec Un Panier

Peinture à l'huile

1882

Nombre 76-13425

36 cm x 48 cm

Acheté en Belgique (Martin — 1967)—reportez-vous à déposer

Condition: bon

Verso: lourde tache d'humidité dans la forme d'araignée

"That's French, right?" asked Camille. "It looks French, but it's so hard to tell in cursive. Everything looks French in cursive, don't you think? I took a French class at school last year, so I know some words—*où est la vache?* Pretty good, huh?"

Art nodded. If he ever needed to locate a *vache*—a cow—he knew whom to ask.

Camille stared at the boy as his eyes ran down the page. "You can read French, can't you?" she said. "I mean, really read it?"

He immediately knew she was right—he could read French. Two minutes ago the thought would never have occurred to him that he could speak any language other than English. But here he was, reading the words in the journal. And it scared him how easy it was. He wasn't just translating the words in his head—he was actually thinking in French.

"So what is this?" the girl asked.

"It's some sort of handwritten inventory," Art said. "Like something an art collector or an art dealer might use."

Camille pointed to the picture of the girl. "So that's a drawing of a painting?" she asked.

"I think so," Art replied. He pointed to the words beneath the image. "The artist's name is Guillou."

"Never heard of him," said Camille.

"Me neither," said Art. He felt as if he was admitting defeat.

"And what's that mess on the right?" she asked.

"The *verso*," he replied. "It means 'reverse.' That's the back of the painting."

"Why would someone want a drawing of the back of a painting?" Camille asked.

"Lots of reasons," replied Art. "Sometimes artists signed or dated their paintings on the back, not the front. Or maybe someone wants to know if a painting has been damaged or repaired. There could be patches on the back of a painting on canvas, or braces on the back of a painting on wood. The back of a painting can tell you a lot about its history."

"So what's on the back of this one?" she asked.

"It's a water stain," replied Art. "The text says it's in the shape of an *araignée*."

"A what?" Camille asked.

"*Araignée*," Art repeated in a perfect French accent. He paused briefly. "In French, it means 'spider.'"

Roper.

Sometimes referred to as the "outside man."

It's a slang term from a rather unique profession — the world of con men.

The roper's job is simple — gain the victims' trust.

Get them to trust you, and then rope them in.

The decision to use the term had been Palmer's idea.

Palmer thought it was cool. He said it sounded retro, like something out of *Ocean's Eleven*.

Winston Lantham, a member of Palmer's team, had initially despised the term.

They weren't con artists, Lantham had insisted. They were professionals—well-trained, well-educated people who took pride in their work.

But Palmer had insisted. It was a perfect description for the role—*embrace it*, he told them.

And so the word had become part of the team's lexicon—one of the unique words that defined their unique jobs.

Over time the term had grown on Lantham. And it turned out that Palmer was right—it was a perfect description.

Everything was now in place. Lantham had left Gleb Bazanov, another member of Palmer's team, set up outside with their SUV. The trap was set. Now it was time for Lantham to do his job.

He straightened his tie and prepared to rope 'em in.

Art meticulously repacked the backpack. He made sure to put the journal back where he had found it—carefully hidden in the lining.

He knew he was making progress in discovering who he was, but it was frustratingly slow. He felt as though there were a dam somewhere in his brain holding back the memories. Every now and then a drop would pop over the dam—a faint afterimage of who he used to be. It was just enough to remind him that another Art—a boy he still didn't know—used to occupy his space.

Camille's voice interrupted his thoughts.

"I think that man's staring at us," she whispered.

Art zipped up the front of his backpack. "What man?" he asked, looking around.

"At the entrance," Camille said under her breath. "The tall guy wearing a tie. Look, but don't look like you're looking."

Art nonchalantly glanced from one side of the entrance hall to the other. He spotted the man instantly. He was tall and thin—dressed neatly in a dark coat and blue tie. He stood out from the small crowd of tourists preparing to leave the museum. And as Camille had noted, he was staring directly at them as he spoke into a cell phone. Art looked down at his backpack and pretended to adjust the straps.

"Let's just head back to the café," Art said. "When I say go, just follow me."

"Too late," Camille responded. "He's—"

Art looked up. The tall man was now standing directly in front of them.

"Are you Camille Sullivan?" the man asked, addressing the girl.

"I'm not supposed to talk to strangers," she replied curtly.

The man smiled. "Of course you aren't," he said. "And you probably weren't supposed to leave the café without your mother's permission either, were you? You had her scared to death."

"Well, I-I . . ." Camille stammered as her faced turned as red as her hair. "She told me to . . . keep an eye on him." She pointed at Art.

"It's okay," the man said. He removed his wallet from his coat pocket and showed them a badge. "I'm Detective Wasberger of the Metropolitan Police. I believe we may have solved the mystery of your friend here."

"Me?" said Art. "You know who I am?"

"I'm not supposed to discuss that," said the man. "Detective Evans thinks it would be best if she had the conversation with you back at the station. She's afraid you might . . ."

"Freak out?" said Art.

The detective nodded. "Yeah, she's worried you might freak out. All I can say," continued the detective, "is that there's a very worried set of parents who lost track of you at Union Station yesterday afternoon."

"The train station!" exclaimed Camille. "C'mon, you have to give us something more than that. Is he from around here? Or maybe New Mexico? Or Idaho? He speaks French — did you know that? Maybe he's Canadian? Or maybe he's French and speaks English really well."

"Not my place to say," replied the detective. "But I

imagine you'll find out soon enough." He pointed to the exit. "We have a car outside," he said. "Your mother's probably already waiting for us."

Camille looked up in alarm. "Is she mad?" she asked. "You know, for leaving the café?"

The detective shrugged. "She's your mom," he said. "Do you think she's mad?"

"Dang," said Camille. "I bet I don't get pizza for an entire year."

The detective laughed. "Don't worry," he said. "I'll tell her you were just doing your job and keeping an eye on your friend. Maybe that will help."

Camille stood up and headed toward the exit. "Trust me," she said. "I will still be in trouble."

Art stood up and threw the backpack over his shoulder. "I got lost at the train station?" he asked.

The detective nodded. "I suspect you gave your parents quite the scare," he said.

The boy started walking toward the exit and then paused. My parents? he thought.

"Something wrong?" asked the detective, who was now several steps ahead of the boy.

Art had no memory of the people he was about to meet—his parents. He didn't know their names, what they looked like, or how they acted. Were they kind like Mary? Were they tall or short? What did they do for a living? Was his father bald, or did he have a head full of hair? Did Art look like his mom or his dad? He could feel the memories pounding against the dam in his head — all the answers, just sitting there somewhere. But the dam holding back those memories held firm. It was all very confusing — and scary. The sudden rush of information made the boy anxious and worried. He felt lightheaded.

Art took a deep breath. He needed to be tough.

"Nothing's wrong," he said to the detective as he hitched up his backpack and continued to the exit.

Camille stood on the granite stoop just outside the tall glass doors of the west entrance to the museum and waited for Art and the detective to catch up. It was turning dark, and the street lamps in front of the museum were illuminated. Halos of icy mist hovered around each light.

"There's the car," the detective said. He pointed toward a large black SUV parked at the far side of the curving driveway that ran in front of the museum entrance. "Let's head on over before we freeze to death."

As they made their way over to the car, a massive man with short-cropped brown hair stepped out of the driver's side and opened the rear door. He wore a pair of incredibly thick round glasses that seemed to sit directly on his eyeballs. He stared at them with a blank expression on his face.

"That's Officer Smith," said Detective Wasberger. Officer Smith nodded at Art and Camille and made an ill-fated attempt at what might have been described as a smile.

Camille stopped and peered inside the back of the car. "Where's my mom?" she asked.

"I'm sure she'll be here any minute," said Detective Wasberger. "Go ahead and grab a seat. It's warm inside."

Camille hesitated. "Maybe I should wait for my mom back in the museum," she said. She glanced at the big man holding the door open for her. She didn't think he looked much like a police officer.

"Your mom will be here any minute," the detective repeated. "Security went to find her. Just go ahead and get in the car."

Something was wrong.

Art glanced over at Camille on the sidewalk and could see that she sensed danger as well. He looked around for a way out, somewhere to run, but he knew that they were trapped. In the quickening darkness, they were little more than shadows—virtually invisible to anyone who might pass by on foot. Art knew that the sound of the traffic —passing just a few feet from where they stood—would instantly muffle any effort to cry out for help.

Art took Camille by the hand. He wanted to kick himself for following the detective out of the museum. He promised himself that if he was able to get out of this mess, he wouldn't trust anyone until his memories had returned.

"What do you want?" he demanded of the so-called detective.

The man smiled. "Just be a good boy and get in the car," he said. The tone of his voice did not match his smile.

Art stood firm. Trust no one, he had decided. "No," he replied steadily.

The detective stepped in closer. He reached into his jacket and pulled out a rectangular black object — about the size of a smartphone. It had two silver electrodes protruding from one end. Art recognized it immediately — it was a stun gun.

The man's smile was now gone.

"Get in the car," he said firmly.

"Art?" asked Camille. "What is that thing?" Her voice was shaky.

"What do you want?" Art repeated. He positioned himself between Camille and the man with the stun gun. The boy held the girl's hand tightly behind his back.

The man pushed a button on the side of the small device. A blue pulse of electricity raced back and forth from one electrode to the other.

Art could hear Camille gasp behind him.

"You're going to help us find something," the man said. "And I'm running out of patience."

Art could feel Camille tighten her grip on his hand. He had no doubt the man would use the device to get what he wanted. The kids had no choice but to get in the car.

CHAPTER 19

6:00 p.m.
Saturday, December 16
West Building, National Gallery of Art,
Washington, DC

Mary Sullivan and the security guard checked every inch of
the gift shop.

There was no sign of Camille or the boy.

"Maybe they headed somewhere else," suggested the
security guard. "Kids get distracted and wander off."

Mary stood in the middle of an aisle and looked around.
She knew that the security guard was trying to be helpful,
but something was wrong. This was not like Camille.

"Can you go ahead and alert the security guards at the
exits?" she asked. Her voice was calm. Her heart was no longer pounding in her chest. She needed to be focused. She
needed to find her child.

"Of course," replied the security guard. "And don't
worry—we always find them."

Mary nodded politely but was not the least bit assured.

* * *

New car smell.

It was the first thought that went through Art's mind as he slid across the back seat of the SUV. They were being kidnapped in the middle of one of the busiest cities in the world, and as strange as it may have seemed, the smell of the car was the first thing the boy had noticed.

Camille followed him into the SUV and settled in next to him. The door shut behind them, and the lock clicked loudly into place. Art tried the handle, but he knew the door wouldn't open.

Camille pulled her seat belt across her body and locked it into place. This act struck Art as somewhat ridiculous under the circumstances.

She glanced over at him but said nothing. He could see the anxiety in her eyes. He buckled his seat belt into place. He didn't know what else to do, and it seemed like a small act of solidarity.

The driver opened the door and dropped his huge frame into the front seat. He pulled his door shut with a thud, then glanced back at the kids in the rearview mirror, his eyes magnified by the thick glasses. Art wondered if he ever blinked.

The front passenger-side door opened and the detective took his seat.

"Let's go," he said as he pulled his door closed. The overhead light blinked off and the interior of the car went dark.

The driver wasted no time. There was a slight click as he turned the key in the ignition and the engine hummed to life. Art was amazed at how quiet it was for such a big vehicle. The SUV pulled onto Seventh Street and headed north.

Detective Wasberger—Art didn't know how else to think of him, although he was pretty sure now the man wasn't a detective and wasn't named Wasberger—turned in his seat and faced the two kids. "Don't even think about trying anything," he said. "It's useless. This vehicle was designed for diplomats. The windows are heavily tinted, so you can wave all you want—no one will see you. Pound on the windows for all I care—the glass is at least an inch thick—bulletproof. You'll break your hand before anyone outside the car hears you."

He paused. Then he looked directly at Art.

"The best thing you can do is sit back and be quiet," the man finally said. "It's a short ride. Be good kids and everything will be fine."

Art knew he was lying. The men, posing as a police officer and a detective, had just kidnapped two kids from the National Gallery of Art. They had not worn masks or made any effort to conceal their identities in any way. The museum had all sorts of security video of Art and Camille talking with this guy, but Detective Wasberger didn't seem the least bit concerned. There was no way the men were simply going to let the kids go. The boy glanced over at Camille. He could see in her face that she understood the dangers as well.

6:06 p.m.
Saturday, December 16
Washington, DC

Dorchek Palmer watched on his iPad as the black SUV carrying the boy and the girl turned onto Seventh Street and headed north. Kidnapping the girl had complicated things, but what choice did they have?

The car moved swiftly from his view on the iPad. He checked the other museum video feeds to make sure there was no sign of the vehicle.

Everything was clear.

The National Gallery's security feed ran on a twenty-four-hour loop. Once the alarm was raised about the disappearance of the boy and the girl—and that would happen any moment—the video would be the first place security and the police would go. Palmer did not intend to allow the feed to reveal anything. He reset the date in the security system for forty-eight hours into the future. Every bit of video taken at the National Gallery over the past twenty-four hours vanished in an instant. He then reset the video feed for the current time and date. Palmer knew that whoever was manning the video panel in the security room would immediately notice that something had happened—a slight blip on the screen. But that didn't matter. There was no way to trace it back to him, and besides, the National Gallery's tech team would probably blame it on some sort of system glitch. The only thing that mattered now was that there was no longer any video evidence that the boy, Palmer, or his team had been at the museum that day.

Palmer smiled. Everything was finally falling into place.

Camille Sullivan had no intention of remaining quiet.

"Why are you doing this?" she asked. Art could hear the anxiety in her voice. She was clearly scared—as was he, but she was still willing to confront the men who had just kidnapped them. Art was impressed.

Neither of the men responded to her question.

The car continued north on Seventh Street.

"Why are you doing this?" she asked again, but with significantly more volume.

Again, she was ignored. The SUV came to a stop at an intersection.

"WHY ARE YOU DOING THIS?" she screamed.

The reaction was immediate. Detective Wasberger snapped around in his seat and faced Camille and Art. He held the stun gun in his right hand, the trigger depressed and blue sparks jumping from the sharp metal points. Art glanced over at Camille. The light from the sparks flickered across her face. The back seat was bathed in a strange blue glow.

"Scream again," he said menacingly to Camille, "and you won't remember the rest of the ride."

Art put his hand on Camille's knee. "It'll be okay," he said.

"Listen to the boy," the detective said. He took his finger off the trigger, and the sparks instantly disappeared. The rear seat of the car went dark once more, and Camille's face retreated into the deep shadows. A faint electrical odor hung in the air—metallic and slightly pungent.

CHAPTER 20

6:12 p.m.
Saturday, December 16
West Building, National Gallery of Art,
Washington, DC

"What do you mean, there's no video?" asked Detective Evans. The frustration was evident in her voice.

Detective Evans had arrived at the National Gallery of Art within minutes of the call from Mary Sullivan. The boy had disappeared, and so had Mary's daughter. The detective's initial reaction had been the same as everyone else's — the kids were probably roaming around the museum somewhere. It was, after all, a massive building. Perhaps they had inadvertently made their way into an administrative area, or maybe they had wandered over to the East Building. But when Detective Evans learned that the entire video feed for the entire museum for the past twenty-four hours had simply disappeared in a blink, she suspected something more was happening.

A security guard sitting before a panel of video monitors shrugged. "I was just sitting here," he said, "watching this kid in a green coat who was getting a little too close to one of the sculptures near the exit. I was about to give a heads-up to the guard when *BAM*, the kid teleports across the room."

"Teleports?" asked the detective.

"Yep, teleports. One second he's next to the sculpture, the next second he's gone. I looked around the room to see if I could find him — and there he was, heading out the exit. He just teleported across the room — like that Nightcrawler character from the comic books. Do you read comic books?"

The detective shook her head. "No."

"Too bad," said the guard. "There's some awesome stuff out there — you should check it out. Anyway, I figured it was some sort of system glitch — maybe a power surge or something. Didn't think anything of it until I got the call that we were looking for a couple of kids. I tried to go back and find them in the café — you know, when they were still with the lady. But there was nothing. Everything was gone. The past twenty-four hours had just disappeared. *POOF.*"

"Has this ever happened before?" asked Detective Evans.

"Not on my watch," replied the guard. "I don't even know how it *could* happen."

Detective Evans thanked the guard and made her way out of the security room and back down the long hallway that led into the public area of the museum. The entire security staff and all the docents had been alerted — everyone

143

was looking for the boy and Camille, which shouldn't have been hard, since the museum was officially closed and all visitors were leaving or already gone. Mary was holding it together—but barely. She was a tough lady.

Within minutes Detective Evans was standing in the middle of the café—the last place the kids had been seen. She remembered her thought from the previous day—how it seemed as if the boy had simply appeared out of thin air in the museum, as if by magic. Now, it seemed, he had disappeared just as mysteriously—and had taken Camille Sullivan with him.

6:19 p.m.
Saturday, December 16
Downtown streets, Washington, DC

Art knew they had to get out of the SUV. He had no idea why they were being kidnapped or by whom, but he suspected it had something to do with whatever memories were swirling behind that dam in his head. One thing was certain—Art did not intend to wait around and find out how these men were going to get to those memories.

The boy had a plan, but he admitted it wasn't a particularly good one, and even worse, it was risky. Still, it was all he had. He reached down to the floor and slowly unzipped his backpack. He pulled out the Coke, placed the can in his lap, and carefully rezipped the backpack.

He glanced over at Camille. He could barely make out her face in the darkness, but he could see that she was watching him. He put his index finger to his lips, signaling her to be quiet. She nodded ever so slightly.

Art took the can in his right hand. He was seated on the passenger side, directly behind the detective. The boy slowly shook the can in his hand. There was a slight splashing noise. Art paused. Neither the driver nor the detective appeared to notice. The boy shook the can a little harder and then paused once more. Again, no one seemed to notice.

Art kept his eyes on the driver and started shaking the can even more vigorously. Suddenly a loud ringing filled the car. Art jumped in his seat. The driver jerked his head to the right and looked over at the detective. It took a moment for Art to realize that the sound was a cell phone. The ringing stopped suddenly. Art could see the detective place the phone to his ear.

"Ten minutes," the man said into the phone. "Maybe fifteen, depending on traffic."

There was a slight pause.

"Got it," he said, and pressed a button to end the call.

The car went silent once more.

Ten or fifteen minutes.

Time was running out.

Art glanced at the road ahead. They were almost half-way down the block and approaching the next intersection.

It was now or never.

Camille had watched as Art retrieved the can of Coke from his backpack and started shaking it. He obviously had something in mind, but what? Art was now looking over the detective's right shoulder at the road ahead.

What is he looking for? she wondered.

Suddenly Art sat back and took the Coke can in both hands.

"Scream," he whispered to her across the back seat.

Scream?

"Scream now!" he yelled.

So she screamed.

CHAPTER 21

6:21 p.m.
Saturday, December 16
Downtown streets, Washington, DC

Art knew Camille could be loud. But he did not appreciate exactly how loud. The sound of Camille's voice exploded in the interior of the SUV like a high-pitched clap of rolling thunder.

The reaction from the front seat was immediate.

The driver's head lurched to the right and his hands followed, sending the vehicle bumping up against the curb. As the driver struggled to regain control of the SUV, the detective snapped around in his seat.

"I warned you!" he yelled.

He swung the stun gun toward Camille, the blue sparks jumping off the sharp metal electrodes.

And that's when Art opened the can of Coke.

Coke, like most other soft drinks, is carbonated. Little bubbles are formed when carbon gas is forced into the liquid. When a can is opened, the little bubbles escape, resulting in a hiss of carbon gas and nothing more. However, if a can is shaken before it is opened, everything changes. The little bubbles form big bubbles, and the result is more than just a slight hiss of carbon gas.

The detective never saw it coming.

The brown liquid exploded from the can. In an instant it covered the detective's stun gun, his arm, and his hand, and drenched the right side of the driver's face. The detective could not react fast enough to pull his finger from the trigger of the stun gun. One hundred thousand volts of electricity followed the conductive path laid down by the stream of soda. The detective's hand twitched as the current ran through it, and rather than releasing the trigger, the man gripped the stun gun even tighter. The blue electrical charge followed the spray of soda across the front seat and to the side of the driver's face. The driver screamed and released the steering wheel. The large SUV careened to the right.

Art could hear the wheels scrape along the curb and see the shocked faces of the pedestrians along the sidewalk. The driver recovered quickly and took control of the steering wheel. However, the detective—who was still clutching the stun gun—pitched to the side and the sharp electrodes planted squarely in the driver's right arm. The driver's whole body suddenly went rigid, and his right foot slammed down on the accelerator. The SUV's wheels screeched as the vehicle lurched forward. The front wheels struck the curb and pushed the SUV sharply to the left. The smell of burned rubber filled the interior of the vehicle.

"Hold on!" Art yelled at Camille.

The SUV shot directly across the street, narrowly missing a small red car traveling in the opposite lane of traffic. The massive vehicle bounced up and over the curb and passed between a light post and trash can. The SUV shredded a short iron fence and crashed headlong into the side of a large stone building. The air bags in the front seat deployed upon impact, and Camille and Art jerked forward violently against their seat belts. A sharp pain shot through Art's right shoulder as his seat belt tightened. Smoke and a burning chemical smell instantly engulfed the interior of the SUV. The rear of the car lifted from the impact and dropped with a thud and a shudder.

Art looked over at Camille. She seemed shaken up but otherwise fine. The same could not be said for the driver and the detective. The detective had somehow ended up across the driver's lap with his left calf wrapped behind the driver's neck. Both men were groaning and appeared barely conscious.

Art and Camille quickly unbuckled their seat belts. Art tried to open his door, but it remained locked. Camille tried her door. Same result. Art knew he would have to open the doors from the front seat. He stretched around the headrest and tried to reach the front door on the passenger side. His right shoulder felt as if it had been hit with a hammer, and he grimaced in pain. Smoke still swirled around in the front seat from the deflated air bags. Art could see that the passenger-side door was bent from the impact.

What if it's broken? he thought.

Art pushed the passenger-side air bag out of the way and pressed down on the door-unlock button. There was a slight buzzing sound.

"Not opening," Camille said from the back seat. "Try again."

The boy pushed the button. Same buzzing sound. Same result. The doors remained locked.

"You're gonna have to try the driver's door!" he said to Camille. The smoke was burning his nose, and he was finding it hard to breathe. They were running out of time.

Camille could see the driver's massive body leaning against the car door. She would have to reach under him to get to the locking mechanism. She hesitated. This would not be easy.

"Do it!" yelled Art. "There's no more time."

Camille reached around the driver's seat and under the driver's thick torso. She had to wedge almost her entire upper body between the driver's door and the seat to get close enough to the lock. The man's armpit was within an inch of her nose. He smelled like cheap lime after-shave and sweat. Camille stretched her hand toward the locking button but was still a couple of inches away. Taking a deep breath, she pushed into the driver's body, burying her nose deep in his armpit. She could no longer see the lock, but she felt around and pushed down. There was a clicking sound from the back seat.

"You did it!" she heard Art exclaim. "Now let's get out of here!"

She heard the door of the SUV open and felt the rush of cold, fresh air into the car.

She was starting to pull her arm back when, suddenly, the driver's massive hand closed around her wrist. The pain was tremendous. Camille wanted to scream, but her face was still buried in the man's armpit.

"You're not going anywhere," the man growled.

She was trapped.

Eric McClain, who had been following the SUV, watched the accident unfold from a half block away. McClain's job was to be available if something went wrong—and something had just gone really wrong.

McClain pulled his car over to the curb and considered what he should do. A small crowd was already starting to gather near the crash site, and smoke was pouring from the front of the SUV. He knew that it would be only a matter of minutes before the police arrived. His sole concern right now was the boy, not the girl or his fellow team members.

The mission was the only thing that mattered—and the mission was to secure the boy.

There was no time to check in with Palmer—events were moving too fast. McClain started to put his car into gear when he saw the boy step out of the back seat.

At least the boy's not hurt, McClain thought.

But the boy was no longer under their control—and that would need to change fast.

It was risky, but McClain would have to grab the boy off the street before the police arrived. Accident scenes were always a state of confusion—smoke, noise, the smell of gasoline in the air, and a gathering crowd—and that commotion would provide McClain with a small window of opportunity. The boy, however, was too big to simply wrestle into the trunk. A stun gun or other obvious weapon was out of the question—it would draw too much attention in the middle of a crowd. But McClain was prepared for this sort of contingency. He opened his glove compartment and pulled out a small blue box. Inside was what appeared to be three cheap retractable ballpoint pens. They were, in fact, devices that fired small tranquilizer darts. Once the trigger —disguised as a pocket clip on each pen—was depressed, the device would fire a tiny dart with a small, almost invisible needle—no more than a quarter inch in length. The devices were virtually silent—compressed air was used to fire the darts. And although the gadgets had an effective range of less than five feet, the substance inside the pens could render a grown man unconscious within seconds. McClain slid all three pens into his coat pocket, put his car into gear, and headed toward the accident scene.

Camille couldn't move—the driver had a vicelike grip on her wrist and had leaned the entire weight of his torso against her. She could feel his chest rising up and down. Her face was still planted firmly in his armpit, and she could barely breathe.

"Let's go!" shouted Art from outside the car. The girl tried to respond, but her words came out muffled.

"Get off me!" the driver barked at the detective. "The boy's getting away!"

Camille heard a groan from the front seat. "What . . . happened?" a groggy voice asked.

"Let's go!" Art shouted again.

There was only one thing Camille could do in her position.

The girl opened her mouth as wide as she could and bit down hard on the man's armpit.

The driver howled in pain. He instantly released his grip on Camille's wrist. She pulled her arm free, slid across the back seat, and was out the door before the driver could react. Art took Camille by the hand, and they started running.

CHAPTER 22

6:25 p.m.
Saturday, December 16
Downtown streets, Washington, DC

He was too late.

Eric McClain was just getting out of his car when the boy and the girl sprinted away from the wreck. He tried to catch up with them, but he was quickly swallowed up in the gathering crowd. He made it through just in time to see the kids disappear around the corner at the end of the block. He thought about chasing them farther, but they had too much of a head start.

McClain knew he needed to act fast, but he also needed help. He made his way to the opposite side of the street to get away from the crowd and placed a call to the two other team members. Luck was on his side — the two had left the museum together but had been delayed in traffic. They were already headed in McClain's direction and would be circling the block within minutes.

"Put in your earpieces," McClain told them before he ended the call. From this point forward all communications would take place using the two-way radio earpiece communicators.

But there was one more call McClain needed to make.

To Palmer.

Art and Camille moved quickly away from the accident scene. As soon as they broke free from the crowd, they sprinted toward the end of the block. They made it around the corner at F Street before stopping along an iron railing. An oval sign on the railing read HOTEL MONACO: WASHINGTON. To their left, just down the sidewalk and less than a hundred feet away, was the entrance to the hotel. It occurred to Art that the car had actually crashed into the side of the hotel, which took up the entire city block. He glanced back down at the entrance to the hotel and saw the parking valets —two young men dressed in matching burgundy outfits —sprinting down the sidewalk directly at Art and Camille. The valets were followed close behind by a portly limousine driver, who seemed to be struggling to keep up the pace. Art's heart jumped in his chest, and he gripped Camille's hand tightly as he prepared to run.

"They're not after us," Camille said calmly. "They're checking on the accident."

She was right.

The valets sprinted past them without a word.

"Evening," the limousine driver gasped as he trundled past the kids.

Art took a deep breath and tried to calm down. He needed to get his bearings. The smoky chemical smell of the air bags still lingered in his nostrils.

The boy looked around. Directly across the street was yet another massive stone building with tall columns. Washington, DC, was filled with structures like that. Large letters on the front identified the building as the National Portrait Gallery. On the far corner of the intersection was a large modern structure covered with glass—a sharp contrast to its stone counterpart across the street. To Art's right, farther down F Street, was a large ornate gold clock that jutted from the side of an old building. The clock read 6:29.

Traffic continued to flow by at a steady pace, but the sidewalks were relatively empty. The sights and sounds of the wreck had drawn in most of the bystanders for a curious and perhaps morbid peek. Art exhaled for what seemed like the first time in forever.

"Are you okay?" he asked Camille.

She nodded. "Are you?"

The boy could hear the sirens in the distance. The police would be there any minute. His shoulder ached from the wreck, and he felt as if he had just run a marathon.

"I'm fine," he replied.

A million different thoughts raced through his head. What did those men want? Where had they been taking him? Was there anyone he could trust? Art tried to push back against the flood of thoughts rushing through his brain, but the tactic wasn't working. He felt as if his head were about to explode.

And that's when Camille started laughing. Everything in his head came to a screeching halt.

Laughing?

"What's so funny?" Art asked. Didn't she understand how serious this situation had become?

Camille continued to laugh. "You . . . with . . . a . . . can of Coke," she finally managed to gasp. "That . . . was . . . hilarious."

"Listen," said Art, "this is a very dangerous—"

"A Coke!" Camille exclaimed, and then doubled over in laughter once more. "How'd you think of that?"

"We don't have time . . ." Art started to say—and then he paused. A slight smile crossed his face. It was ridiculous, he realized. The fact that it had actually worked made it even more so.

Art smiled wider. "How did the driver taste?"

"Terrible," Camille said. "Like old socks."

The phone call had gone just as Eric McClain had expected. Palmer had exploded when he learned that the boy had gotten away—again. But Palmer was Palmer—and after threatening to fire the entire team, he calmed down and formulated a plan. Palmer instructed McClain to stay and keep an eye on the accident scene in case the boy returned. The other team members would start searching for the boy and the girl. They couldn't have gotten far—it was dark, starting to snow, and turning colder by the minute. Palmer figured the kids would probably try to make contact with the girl's mother or the police. Palmer would monitor the mother's phone and police communications. If the two called for help, the team would intercept before anyone arrived. There was still no indication that the boy knew who he was or why they were after him. But Palmer's luck wouldn't hold out forever.

"Find them," Palmer had said to his search party. "Do whatever you have to do."

McClain could hear the police sirens getting closer. He was staying near the accident scene, just as Palmer had told him to do. If the boy showed up again, McClain needed to be in a position to seize him. But from his vantage point in the middle of the block, McClain had a limited view of the surrounding area.

He pulled his coat tight and headed up the sidewalk.

"Now what?" asked Camille. "Wait for the police and let 'em know what happened?"

"No," replied Art.

"No?"

"We can't trust anyone," he said.

"What does that mean?" asked Camille.

"It means that someone who claimed to be a detective just kidnapped us. He had a badge—didn't you see it? How do we know he wasn't a real detective? What if we walk back around that corner and get stuffed into another car? I don't know who I can trust, and I'm not taking any chances."

"You can trust my mom," said Camille. "We can use the phone at the hotel to call her."

"I trust your mom," said Art. "And I trust you. But that isn't the problem. Somehow the two guys in the car knew I was at the museum. Think about it—the detective said that you had left the café without telling your mom. How could he have known that? How long have they been watching us? How many of them are there? I'll bet anything that they know where you and your mom live. They might even have followed us from your house, or tapped your phone, or both. You can't call your mom while I'm around."

The boy paused.

"Besides," he finally said, "I've got something I need to do."

"What?" asked Camille.

Art held out his backpack. "I now have a bunch of clues," he said. "And I'm going to find out who I am and why those guys are after me."

CHAPTER 23

6:32 p.m.
Saturday, December 16
Downtown streets, Washington, DC

"Clues?" asked Camille incredulously. "What are you talking about? Your backpack was full of a bunch of junk."

"The receipt from the coffee shop," said Art. "That's a clue."

"The receipt?" replied Camille. "That's your big clue? You had a croissant and a hot chocolate. Mystery solved."

"You don't get it, do you?" Art asked.

"Get what? It's just a piece of paper."

"Do you ever go out for breakfast?" he asked. "Just you and your mom?"

"Sure," replied Camille. "Almost every Sunday morning, we go to this little restaurant right down . . ."

Camille paused. A smile crossed her face.

"Every Sunday morning," she began again, "we walk to the same little restaurant. It's right down the street from our house."

"Exactly," said Art. "You don't drive across town for

breakfast — you go somewhere close to home. And maybe I did the same thing. Maybe I live near the coffeehouse and I go there with my parents all the time. Or maybe I was staying at a hotel close to the place, or maybe I was just passing through. Who knows? But it seems as good a place to start as any other."

Art was right — it was a good place to start. But what if it led nowhere? What if it was simply a dead end? Camille was cold, and it was starting to snow. She knew her mother was worried to death. Everything about this seemed like a bad idea. But for the first time since she had met Art, he seemed to have a purpose — a goal. Camille could begin to see something more than the quiet boy who had arrived at her home the previous night. He no longer seemed completely lost.

"Well," she said, "I guess we'd better find that coffee shop."

"You're not going to the coffee shop," replied Art.

"What?!" exclaimed Camille.

"I'm going there alone," he said. "They're after me, not you. Give me a head start, and then you can go to the hotel and call your mom. Even if your mom's phone is tapped, I'll be long gone by the time she gets there — and you'll be safe at the hotel."

"Not a chance," said Camille. "I made a promise."

"A promise?"

"To my mom—to watch out for you."

Part of the boy wanted to laugh at this short red-haired girl and her promise to watch out for him. But he didn't. She was tough and brave, and Art trusted her. And to be honest, he could probably use a friend.

Eric McClain made it to the corner of Seventh Street and F Street just as the police cars arrived and headed toward the accident scene. The blue flashing lights filled the inter-section. He looked back and watched the crowd surround-ing the smashed vehicle move aside as the police cars approached.

McClain turned his attention back to his post. He glanced to his left, directly down F Street, the direction in which the kids had escaped.

Holy cow.

It took every bit of self-control not to react.

There they were—the boy and the girl—standing by a short iron railing just across the street and less than one hundred feet away. McClain turned away so the kids would not see him staring at them. He immediately notified the other team members, whose car was now within two blocks of the intersection. He quickly laid out his plan. Regina Cash would get dropped off at the opposite end of the block on Eighth Street. Nigel Stenhouse, the final member of the team, would park directly across the street from the Hotel Monaco and in front of the National Portrait Gallery. They would have the block completely sealed off. McClain would then approach the boy and the girl and subdue them with the tranquilizer darts. Stenhouse would converge with the car; they would pop both kids into the back seat and take off. It could be done in five seconds — perhaps fewer. They would pick up Regina a block away and head back to base.

Simple.

McClain nonchalantly glanced over his shoulder. The boy and the girl were still standing there.

Stupid kids, he thought. How did Lantham and Bazanov let those two get away?

McClain received the signal that Nigel Stenhouse and Regina Cash were in place.

Showtime.

Mary Sullivan sat in the front seat of the detective's car and stared out the window. They were driving slowly down Madison Drive, just south of the museum. Detective Evans had explained that it was still too soon to put out an alert for Camille and the boy. They had been gone for only an hour, and it wasn't the first time that a couple of kids had wandered off by themselves. There were certainly plenty of things to see in the area around the National Gallery of Art — things that might draw the attention of a couple of tweens. The normal protocol was to check the area around the museum before putting out any alerts. Mary knew this procedure made sense. But she also knew that Camille would not have left the museum without her permission. Something else was going on—and Mary suspected that Detective Evans felt the same way. Mary had begged her to do something—anything.

It didn't take a whole lot of convincing.

Although she couldn't issue a formal missing-child alert, Detective Evans had asked a couple of patrol officers in the area around the museum for a favor. She provided them with a description of Camille and Art and asked them to let her know if they spotted the kids. The officers readily agreed—they understood how the procedures worked, but they were also parents. They would keep an eye out for the kids.

The call came just as Detective Evans and Mary Sullivan reached the intersection with Twelfth Street. It was from one of the patrol officers. The detective listened as the officer spoke.

"Thanks," the detective said. "Heading that way now."

She ended the call and turned to Mary. "Car crash on Seventh Street, just a few blocks from the museum. Witnesses reported two kids running from the scene of the accident."

The detective paused.

"One of them," she finally continued, "was described as a young girl with bright red hair and wearing a polka dot jacket."

"Camille!" Mary exclaimed. "A car accident? How?"

"We'll figure that out later," said the detective. "Let's just find your daughter and the boy."

Detective Evans turned onto Twelfth Street and headed north.

CHAPTER 24

6:43 p.m.
Saturday, December 16
Downtown streets, Washington, DC

Eric McClain waited for the light to change and then started walking across the intersection. The other team members had now assumed their places. Regina Cash stood at the far end of the block on Eighth Street, and McClain could see the large black SUV idling directly across the street in front of the National Portrait Gallery.

Everything was going as planned.

The boy was talking, and the girl had her back to McClain. They appeared oblivious to what was going on around them. McClain gripped the knockout pens in his right coat pocket. All he needed was a second to incapacitate both of the kids. They would never even see it coming.

The black SUV pulled away from the front of the National Portrait Gallery and slowly headed toward the rendezvous point.

McClain glanced once again at the boy and the girl.

The boy was no longer talking. He was staring directly

at McClain. They locked eyes for only a moment, but that was all it took.

"We're going to need a taxi," said Camille. "It's too cold to walk to the coffee shop."

Art didn't respond.

"Didn't you hear me?" she said. "We're going to need a taxi."

Again, Art didn't respond. He had just locked eyes with a man in a long gray coat on the crosswalk at the intersection. It had been for only a moment, and the man had looked away just as Art caught his eye. But Art knew something was wrong.

"Run," Art said.

"What?"

The man was now staring directly at Art. The pretense was gone.

"Run!" the boy yelled again as he grabbed Camille by the hand and started pulling her down the sidewalk. They had a decent head start, and Art hoped that they would be able to outrun their pursuer. But that hope quickly evaporated. Up ahead—past the stairs leading to the entrance to the hotel—a woman in a light brown jacket was now sprinting toward them. To his right Art spied a large black SUV heading directly at them from across the street. It was identical to the vehicle from which the kids had just escaped.

How many of these guys are there? the boy wondered.

And do they drive anything other than black SUVs?

Art realized that the sidewalk had become a trap. That left only one option.

"The hotel!" he yelled at Camille. "We have to get to the hotel!"

CHAPTER 25

6:46 p.m.
Saturday, December 16
Downtown streets, Washington, DC

People were converging on them from all directions.

Art could hear the footsteps behind him growing louder, and the woman in the light brown jacket was closing the distance fast.

"Run!" he yelled again.

The boy and girl made it to the base of the stairs leading to the entrance to the hotel and started climbing. Their pursuers, however, had closed the gap to within a few yards. Camille's short legs could cover only one step at a time, and Art knew it would be only a matter of seconds before their pursuers would be on them.

Camille's heart was pounding in her chest. Art had moved quickly ahead of her and was now standing at the entrance to the hotel, urging her to hurry. She had almost made it to the top of the stairs when she felt a tug on the back of her coat. She tipped backwards on her heels.

"Gotcha!" a man's voice exclaimed from behind her.

But she did not intend to be caught that easily. Camille threw her arms backwards and slipped from her coat. She glanced behind her just in time to see the man stumble back down the steps, her coat still in his grip. Camille bounded up the last two steps to the entrance to the hotel.

Art and Camille burst through the doors of the hotel and into the lobby.

The smell of cloves, pine needles, and oranges filled the room. Thick strands of evergreen garland strung with white twinkling lights hung everywhere, and a massive Christmas tree adorned with purple and gold ornaments stood in the middle of the lobby.

"Run!" Art yelled at Camille, and pointed to a wide set of stairs to their right.

But Camille did not run.

Next to the lobby doors was a tall brass umbrella stand. Camille grabbed an umbrella from the holder and thrust it through the handles of the lobby doors, like a makeshift dead bolt.

Art was impressed. The umbrella wouldn't hold their pursuers back for long, but it might buy them just enough time to get away.

* * *

6:48 p.m.
Saturday, December 16
Hotel Monaco, Washington, DC

James Appleton was a small, fussy man, which made him the perfect person to run the Hotel Monaco. He expected everything to be perfect. He expected all employees to be at their posts. He expected all guests to have a perfect experience at his hotel. But right now things were not as he expected, and Appleton was in crisis mode.

A massive SUV had crashed into the east side of his hotel just twenty minutes ago. A large crowd—including many of his employees—had gathered by the windows on the east side of the lobby and were watching the scene unfold outside. As of now, the valet stand, concierge desk, and bell stand were unmanned. One floor up, in one of the hotel's ballrooms, the American Font Association's Christmas ball had just gotten under way. Appleton grimaced at the thought of the flashing lights and sirens right outside the windows of the ballroom. A party at the Hotel Monaco was not a cheap endeavor, and Appleton knew that the American Font Association, a notoriously fastidious group, expected everything—everything—to be perfect. Appleton decided that he had better head outside to make sure the police handled the accident as quickly as possible.

Heading toward the front door of the hotel, Appleton

noticed two kids sprinting from the entrance toward the grand staircase. He was starting to yell at them when he noticed the front door: the two juvenile delinquents had barred the doors to his hotel with an umbrella. Outraged, Appleton yelled for security, realizing almost immediately that his entire security team was standing next to the window on the far side of the room watching the action outside.

I'll take care of this myself, Appleton fumed as he headed across the lobby toward the front doors.

Regina Cash managed to grab McClain before he could tumble down the stairs to the sidewalk below.

"I'm starting to hate these kids," he growled.

He threw the girl's coat to the ground and sprinted up the stairs to the entrance to the hotel. He pushed on the doors, but they didn't budge.

He pulled. The doors still didn't budge.

McClain looked through the glass on the front of the entrances. Someone had inserted an umbrella through the door handles.

There was no time to waste.

"Stand back," McClain said to Cash. "I'm going to bust through."

He backed up as far as he could on the small landing, took a deep breath, and sprinted toward the double front doors.

* * *

James Appleton reached the front doors of the hotel, grabbed the umbrella, and pulled it from the handles.

Appleton went to throw open the doors. He had a few choice words for the police officers at the scene of the accident outside.

Eric McClain braced for the impact with the double doors.

But instead of hitting the hard brass frames, he found only air.

As soon as Appleton had flung the doors wide open, a man flew past him and into the lobby of the hotel. Off balance, the man tripped down a small set of marble steps, stumbled uncontrollably across the lobby, and crashed into the bottom of the hotel's massive Christmas tree.

Appleton gasped.

The tree teetered ever so slightly, and for a moment, Appleton thought it might remain upright.

But the tree fell—slowly and majestically. The evergreen hit the marble floor with a thud and a whoosh. Tinsel, strings of lights, and pine needles flew everywhere. Glass ornaments exploded throughout the lobby.

The large crowd that had gathered to watch the accident scene through the windows now turned in unison toward the events unfolding in the middle of the hotel.

One man held up a drink and yelled: "Timber!"

The crowd erupted in laughter.

CHAPTER 26

6:52 p.m.
Saturday, December 16
Hotel Monaco, Washington, DC

Regina Cash stared at the enormous Christmas tree splayed across the floor of the lobby and directly on top of Eric McClain.

"Do you think he's dead?" one of the guests in the lobby asked.

"Hard to tell," said someone else.

"Do we need a chain saw?" asked a third person.

A moan emanated from somewhere deep within the mass of branches, pine needles, ornaments, and tinsel.

Regina Cash did not have time to dig McClain out from under the tree. She had just spotted the boy and the girl at the top of the stairs to her right. Cash contacted Nigel Stenhouse. It was now up to them.

Art and Camille made it to the top of the stairs and onto a broad landing overlooking the lobby. Nicely dressed men and women milled about the second floor with drinks in their hands—no one seemed to be paying attention to the two kids. The high walls were painted gold and covered with large mirrors and massive paintings. Just like the lobby below, the landing was decorated to the hilt for the holiday season—garland, lights, and wreaths hung everywhere. At the far end of the landing was a wide hallway. A sign above the entrance to the corridor read CONFERENCE FACILITIES AND BALLROOMS.

Art pointed toward the hallway. "That way," he said.

CHAPTER 27

6:54 p.m.
Saturday, December 16
Hotel Monaco, Washington, DC

Regina Cash spotted the boy and the girl as soon as she hit the top of the stairs. The kids had a respectable lead—they had just entered the long hallway leading to the conference facilities and ballrooms. Cash sprinted across the landing to the entrance to the corridor. The passageway was well lit —the kids would see her coming from a mile away. Cash quickly located a panel of light switches just inside the hallway. It was time to turn the circumstances to her advantage.

The bright lights in the hallway dimmed suddenly.

"Uh-oh," said Camille.

Art glanced behind them. The middle of the hallway remained reasonably well lit, but along the walls there were simply dark shapes and shadows.

"Be cool," Camille said. She tugged on Art's arm to slow his pace. The hallway had grown increasingly crowded as they made their way. They moved quickly but tried not to run so as to avoid drawing any attention to themselves.

Up ahead, at the end of the corridor, was a large mirror that seemed to take up most of the wall. Art looked in the mirror for any sign of their pursuers coming up from behind. Again, nothing but dark shapes and shadows along the walls. That worried him.

A large arrow on the wall next to the mirror pointed to the left. PARIS BALLROOM, the sign read. More important, a rectangular box near the ceiling pointed in the same direction—bright-red glowing letters spelled out EXIT.

"I guess I know which way we're heading," Camille said.

Art nodded and then glanced back over his shoulder. It was still impossible to make out any details in the darkened hallway, but he knew their pursuers were back there somewhere.

"Let's go," he said. They turned the corner and headed toward the ballroom and the exit.

They found the corridor outside the ballroom packed with people. White-coated servers with platters of appetizers bobbed and weaved between dark-suited men and women in dresses. Art and Camille immediately spotted another rectangular box on the far side of the crowded hallway. This one had no arrows. It read simply EXIT, indicating a door leading to a stairwell.

Camille didn't hesitate. "We're going in," she said as she

grabbed Art by the hand and pulled him into the middle of the crowd.

"Excuse me, coming through," Camille said over and over again as she squeezed herself and the boy through the crowd.

In less than a minute they had reached the far side of the room and stood beneath the exit sign. The stairway was directly in front of them.

"Down the steps and we're out of here," said Camille triumphantly.

Art stepped over to the window next to the door and peered down at the road below. He motioned Camille over and pointed outside. Directly across the street was a large black SUV.

"They're waiting for us," he said.

Camille pounded her fist on the wall. "They're everywhere!" she wailed. "How are we going to get out of here?"

Art looked back at the crowd standing in front of the ballroom for any sign of the pursuers. He found little more than dark silhouettes and indistinct faces. He still had no idea how many people were after them—or why.

It was only a matter of time before the pursuers caught up to them. If the boy and girl were going to get out of the hotel, they would have to do something drastic.

Art turned to Camille. "I changed my mind," he said. "We're going down the stairs."

CHAPTER 28

6:58 p.m.
Saturday, December 16
Hotel Monaco, Washington, DC

"You're kidding, right?" asked Camille as they stepped inside the stairwell. "There could be twenty of them waiting for us out there."

"I'm not kidding," Art replied. "We're going to walk right out the exit."

Camille stared at him.

He's lost it completely, she thought.

Art took off his jacket and handed it to her. "It's cold outside," he said.

Camille took the jacket and slipped it on. Her mom was going to be furious that Camille had lost her red jacket with the white polka dots.

Art opened his backpack and took out his Yankees cap. "Put it on," he said. "Your red hair can be seen from a mile away."

The girl took the cap and snuggled it down over her mound of red hair.

"Just walk right out the exit?" she asked. "That's your plan?"

"Yep," the boy replied. "That's my plan."

Art pointed at a small box on the stairwell wall—just next to the door leading back into the ballroom hallway.

Camille smiled.

Regina Cash made her way over to the window and stared down at the sidewalk below. She could see the SUV parked across the street. She knew that Nigel Stenhouse was waiting for the kids somewhere outside the emergency exit, figuring they wouldn't dare to go out the front door of the hotel.

But there was no sign of the kids.

Be patient, she told herself. Everything's going according to plan.

And that's when it happened.

Up and down the entire hallway, small strobe lights near the ceiling started flashing. Immediately the multitude of conversations in the hallway stopped. No one seemed to know what was happening.

No one but Regina Cash.

I really hate those kids, she thought.

Cash covered her ears with her hands. She knew what was coming next.

The noise started a moment later—a high-pitched, pulsating sound.

Briefly, the crowd remained frozen in place, uncertain

what to do. Then someone in the throng yelled, "Fire!" and in an instant, everyone rushed toward the exit sign.

As soon as he pulled the small red lever, Art moved away from the door. Lights immediately started flashing in the stairway, followed by the piercing sounds of the fire alarm. Art and Camille covered their ears. In the confined space of the stairwell, the noise seemed unbearably loud. Art kept his eye on the door, waiting for the crowd to appear. But there was nothing — just the sound and the flashing lights. Had his plan not worked?

Where is everybody? he wondered. He looked anxiously at Camille, who seemed to be thinking the same thing.

And then, suddenly, the exit door burst open. The stairwell filled with people, who started filing down the stairs toward the emergency exit.

Camille grinned at Art, who smiled back.

They squeezed into the crowd heading downstairs.

7:02 p.m.
Saturday, December 16
Downtown streets, Washington, DC

Nigel Stenhouse ripped the receiver from his ear. The piercing noise had almost burst his eardrum. He had been waiting outside with his eyes peeled on the emergency exit door when the noise started. Stenhouse, looking up at the windows of the hotel, saw the flashing lights and instantly recognized what was happening.

Someone had pulled a fire alarm.

Smart kids, he thought. Regina should have been more careful.

He knew that the plan would have to change. Within a few seconds, a crowd of people would start pouring out the exit. And somewhere in that mob was a young boy who held the key to a massive fortune.

Things were about to get exciting.

Stenhouse took a position just to the side of the exit door and prepared to act. He would have to move quickly —identify the kid in the masses, grab him, and move him to the SUV by any means necessary. It wasn't the best of circumstances, but the noise and confusion of the crowd would provide some cover. The team couldn't let the boy get away yet again—there was too much at stake.

Stenhouse pressed his back against the stone exterior of the hotel. His frosty breath drifted out into the night. For a moment, the only noise was the muffled sound of the fire alarm from inside the building. The exit door remained closed.

A few seconds passed, and nothing happened.

Stenhouse wondered whether everyone had been shuttled to another exit—perhaps through the front of the hotel?

And then the door creaked open ever so slightly. It seemed to pause in that position. Stenhouse readied himself. For a moment, everything was still.

Then the door exploded wide open. The muffled sound of the fire alarm gave way to a full-throttle blare. People poured out in waves. Stenhouse tried to maintain his position by the door, but the crowd was too thick and moving too fast. The man soon found himself standing in the middle of the street at the far edge of the mob.

Surrounded by a throng of people, Art and Camille squeezed through the exit door and onto the sidewalk. Art had forgotten how bitterly cold it was outside. A light snow continued to fall. The crowd of partiers, however, did not seem the least bit deterred by the fire alarm or the cold or the snow — in fact, it was as if they had simply moved the festivities outdoors. The sidewalk next to the hotel was filled with people who mingled about with drinks in hand. No one seemed to notice, or care, that the temperature was well below freezing.

Art spotted the black SUV he had seen from the window on the second floor. He could see the exhaust pouring from the rear of the vehicle.

He and Camille needed to get out of there, and fast.

To his right Art could see the massive stone façade of the National Portrait Gallery. Heading that way was out of the question — he and Camille had almost been cornered by their pursuers in that area, and for all Art knew, some of them remained there. The kids would need to head in the opposite direction.

He got Camille's attention and pointed to their left. Camille nodded her understanding.

Regina Cash spotted them. The kids stood on the far side of the crowd to her left, no more than twenty feet away. The girl was now wearing the boy's coat and a hat.

Not much of a disguise, Cash thought.

She looked around for any sign of Nigel Stenhouse but couldn't see him in the large crowd. She tried contacting him on her two-way radio, but the only thing she heard in her earpiece was static.

She would have to handle this herself.

Don't rush, Regina cautioned herself. *Let the kids make the first move. Just watch and wait for the right opportunity.*

Her patience paid off. Instead of sticking to the safety of the crowd, the kids broke free and started walking south along the sidewalk.

CHAPTER 29

7:07 p.m.
Saturday, December 16
Downtown streets, Washington, DC

A long line of cars were parked along Eighth Street just outside the Hotel Monaco. Regina Cash realized that the vehicles would provide the perfect cover for catching up to and overtaking the kids. She pushed through the crowd and quickly made her way into the street, over to a small blue car. Using the car to conceal herself, Cash lifted her head ever so slightly and peeked through the window. On the other side of the vehicle, she could see the boy and the girl moving quickly along the wide tree-lined sidewalk. They had a bit of a lead, but the distance was manageable. Cash knew she would have to move fast to reach them. She glanced around for any sign of Nigel Stenhouse, but he was nowhere to be seen. She reached into her coat and withdrew a small air pistol that fired a tranquilizer dart. Cash would have one shot to subdue the boy. Once that happened, the girl would have no choice but to cooperate.

Keeping her head low, Cash sprinted from one car to

the next, glancing up occasionally to make sure the kids had not changed course or stopped.

Finally, Cash arrived at a large white sedan. She peeked once again through the windows and realized she was almost parallel with the boy and the girl. They were less than fifty feet from the end of the block. She couldn't allow them to reach the intersection. It was now or never.

Just a few feet ahead of the kids was the service entrance to the hotel—a dark recessed space adjacent to the sidewalk. It was the perfect place for an ambush. Cash gripped the pistol tightly with her finger on the trigger. She was a crack shot—she never missed. The boy didn't stand a chance.

Cash stepped around the white sedan, leveled the pistol at the boy, and prepared to fire.

They were almost to the end of the block. Art glanced back over his shoulder. So far so good—no one seemed to be following them. Just a bit more, and they would reach the corner of E Street. From there, they could catch a cab and be far away from the hotel in a matter of minutes.

"You look cold," said Camille.

"I'll be okay," Art assured her. "Besides, I think we've lost them."

The words had barely left his mouth when he saw her —standing behind Camille, next to a large white car parked in the street. It was the woman in the brown jacket. She was pointing something at the boy—a gun of some sort.

Art had no time to react. There was a slight pop of air, and a small red dart implanted itself firmly in the thickly padded shoulder strap of his backpack. Art looked down —the dart had missed hitting his chest by less than an inch.

Startled by the small red dart that had suddenly appeared on the strap of Art's backpack, Camille grabbed the dart and held it between her fingers. A tiny drop of milky liquid clung to the tip of the projectile.

Regina Cash stared in disbelief.

It had been a perfect shot, and yet—miraculously—the boy had been saved by the shoulder strap on his backpack.

The element of surprise was gone, and there was no time to load another tranquilizer dart. Cash would have to do this the hard way. She sprinted from the side of the car directly at the boy and the girl. Covering the distance in three quick strides, Cash pushed the kids toward the dark recess in the side of the hotel.

CHAPTER 30

Later, after waking up, Regina Cash would try to put the pieces together.

She remembered running across the sidewalk.

She remembered shoving the boy and the girl toward the service entrance of the hotel.

She remembered the shocked look on the boy's face.

She remembered the girl yelling at her to stop.

She remembered thinking that Dorchek Palmer would be very pleased.

She remembered thinking that she was going to be very, very rich.

And she remembered a sudden, sharp pain in the side of her neck.

After that the memories ceased. There was only darkness.

She woke up an hour later, lying in the dark recesses of the service entrance at the Hotel Monaco with a small red dart in the side of her neck and a pounding headache.

* * *

7:16 p.m.

Saturday, December 16

Downtown streets, Washington, DC

"Camille?"

No answer.

"Camille?" Art asked again. The light from the sidewalk penetrated just a few feet into the recess in which he now stood. The lady in the brown jacket lay on the ground at his feet. He could see her chest rising and falling as she breathed —small frosty clouds drifting from her open mouth. But he didn't see Camille.

"Camille?" he asked once more.

"Art?" Camille finally responded from the darkness. "What just happened?"

"I'm . . . not sure," he replied. "We were walking down the sidewalk and then the woman in the brown jacket appeared. She had a gun and . . . well, then we're here."

"Where's 'here'?" asked Camille.

Art noticed a small sign on the wall. "Service entrance to the hotel," he said.

Camille stepped out of the darkness and knelt by the woman lying on the ground. A red dart protruded from the side of her neck. In the woman's hand was a small pistol.

"I wish my mom had let me have a phone," said Camille.

Art strode over and put his hand on the girl's shoulder. He knew this wasn't easy on her.

"We'll call her soon. I promise."

"Call her?" said Camille. "Are you kidding? I want a picture of this! Nobody's ever going to believe me. Do you know how exciting this is? I had that little dart in my hand —I had no idea what it was. I mean, I knew it was a dart. But what was it doing on your backpack, you know? So I was just looking at it when she shoved us. I didn't even think —I just jabbed. Next thing I know, she's on the ground. It's like we're secret agents or something."

Art smiled. It was exciting—and ridiculous, and stupid, and incredibly dangerous. And they still had no idea why all these people were following them, or how many more might be out there.

"Let's go," Art said as he stepped around the woman. "I don't want to be hanging around if more of these guys show up."

Art peeked around the corner. The fire alarm had stopped, and he could see people filing back into the hotel at the far end of the block. "Coast is clear," he said. "Follow me."

Art and Camille stepped out of the service entrance, turned left, and continued quickly down the block until they reached E Street.

"There!" Camille said. She pointed at a taxi parked along the side of the street.

Art took one last glance back up the sidewalk and then followed Camille to the cab.

Nigel Stenhouse stood across the street from the Hotel Monaco's emergency exit. The fire alarm had finally stopped blaring, and the crowd was beginning to funnel back into the hotel. He put his earpiece back into place.

"Regina? Eric?" he said. "Any sign of the kids?"

There was no answer—just static.

Stenhouse made his way across the street and stood next to the door leading back into the hotel. He kept a close eye on the rapidly thinning crowd, but there was no sign of the boy or the girl—or Eric McClain or Regina Cash.

It was as if they had all simply disappeared into thin air.

He tried contacting Regina Cash on her cell phone, but there was no response.

Stenhouse had no choice—he placed a call to Dorchek Palmer.

"Report," Palmer said when he answered the phone.

Stenhouse grimaced. "No sign of the boy or girl," he replied.

There was silence on the other end of the line.

"Did you hear me?" Stenhouse asked.

"I heard you," Palmer said calmly. "What happened?"

"I'm not sure," replied Stenhouse. "And I can't locate McClain or Cash, either."

Silence again. Stenhouse suspected Palmer was trying

to track down his teammates. Palmer had ways of doing things like that.

"I tracked Regina's phone," Palmer finally said. "She's somewhere near the hotel just south of you."

Stenhouse turned and started making his way down the street. "On my way," he said.

After a hundred feet or so, Stenhouse could just make out a dark opening on the side of the hotel. It was a narrow space — carefully hidden in the wall of the massive stone building.

"I think I found a service entrance," he said to Palmer, who did not respond.

Stenhouse quickened his pace. Moments later he turned the corner into the darkened passageway. It took his eyes a moment to adjust to the darkness.

"Well?" asked Dorchek Palmer.

"We have a problem," replied Stenhouse. "I just sent you a picture."

A moment later Palmer's phone pinged. He opened the text message and looked at the photo that Stenhouse had sent.

For the third time that day, Palmer was caught off-guard.

Stenhouse had sent him a photograph of Regina Cash, one of the most highly trained covert operatives in the world, lying unconscious on the ground.

"No sign of the kids," said Stenhouse. "They're still loose in the city."

Camille opened the rear door of the taxi and climbed into the back seat. Her heart was beating a mile a minute. She glanced back to make sure no one was following them, but everything looked clear. Art followed her into the cab and pulled the door shut.

The taxi driver, a heavy middle-aged man who had not shaved for several days and smelled like stale coffee and corn flakes, turned and looked at them. "Little young to be catchin' a taxi, aren't ya?" he asked gruffly.

"Not that young," snapped Camille. She was quickly running out of patience with adults.

"Taxis cost money," replied the driver. "And I ain't no babysitter. So get out and go call your parents to come get you."

Art pulled three twenty-dollar bills out of his backpack and held them up. "Will this work?" he asked.

The driver contemplated the currency held between Art's fingers.

"Don't forget to tip," the man said as he put the car into gear. "So where we headed?"

Art read the address from the coffeehouse receipt. The taxi pulled away from the curb and headed west along E Street.

Camille glanced out the rear window of the taxi. "Do you think there's more of them?" she asked.

"I'd bet on it," replied Art.

Camille sighed and settled back in her seat. "I was afraid you were going to say that."

CHAPTER 31

7:22 p.m.
Saturday, December 16
Downtown streets, Washington, DC

Detective Evans surveyed the chaos. Three police cars and a fire truck sat parked in the middle of Seventh Street, their flashing lights strobing the entire area. A wrecker was trying to maneuver into place as a crowd continued to mill around the accident. The SUV had yet to be moved, and its crumpled front end remained smashed against the side of the Hotel Monaco. The smell of burning oil hovered in the air. As if to make things worse, a fire alarm had gone off in the hotel, sending hundreds of people pouring into the street. The alarm had finally ended, but much of the crowd had yet to go away, many of them coming over to this side of the building to check out the accident. And to top things off, it was turning colder and the snow was picking up.

"Like I mentioned on the radio," said Officer Jake Roberts, a twenty-something traffic cop with two years under his belt, "one witness swore that he saw two kids — one with bright red hair and a polka dot jacket — jump out of the car and take off down the sidewalk." The officer gestured in the direction of F Street.

Detective Evans glanced toward the sidewalk. "Anyone else see them?" she asked.

"No, ma'am," replied the officer. "But you know how it is with things like this—lots of smoke and confusion. No one's really sure what they saw or what happened."

The detective nodded. "Notify the other units to be on the alert for a girl with red hair wearing a red jacket with white polka dots. She's probably with a blond boy in a blue jacket. If she's trying to get home, she'll head toward Dupont Circle."

"Got it," replied the officer.

Detective Evans walked back to the car where Mary Sullivan stood waiting.

"Well?" asked Mary.

"They were definitely here," said the detective. "They were last seen heading north toward F Street."

"What are we waiting for?" said Mary. "Let's go after them."

"You should really go home and wait there," said the detective. "They might be heading in that direction."

"My sister's going to my house," said Mary. "She'll be there in case Camille shows up or calls."

"Listen," Detective Evans tried again, "I really think you should—"

Mary Sullivan cut off the detective before she could

finish her sentence. "My daughter is somewhere in this city, and I will not go home until I find her. Understood?"

Detective Evans did understand. She would have done the same thing if it had been her child. "Understood," she replied. "Let's go find them."

Detective Evans and Mary Sullivan were turning to get into the detective's car when a short man dressed in a suit stepped in front of them. "Are you in charge?" he demanded in a high-pitched voice.

Evans pointed at a police officer assisting the tow-truck driver. "Actually," she said, "the officer in charge of the accident scene is—"

"That police officer is just a kid!" screamed the man, whose face had turned a bright crimson. "He barely looks like he shaves. I demand to speak to someone in authority! I want someone who can make decisions! I WANT ANSWERS!"

The man looked as if the blood vessels in his temples were going to explode at any moment.

The detective sighed. "Okay," she said, "you're speaking to someone in authority, so calm down. I'm Detective Evans —what seems to be the problem?"

"Problem?" said the man as he waved his arms around wildly. "Are you blind? All of this is the problem. I'm James Appleton, manager of the Hotel Monaco, and this is completely, totally unacceptable. All of this noise and the lights —you're absolutely ruining the night for my guests!"

"I can't control where a wreck happens," explained the

detective. "As you can see, we're trying to get it cleared as quickly as possible. And the fire alarm in your hotel wasn't helping, you know."

"It's those two kids!" screamed Appleton hysterically. "I just know it. They probably had something to do with that wreck. They've already destroyed my lobby, and now they've —"

"Kids?" It was Mary Sullivan. She was standing next to the passenger-side door of the detective's car. "Did you say 'kids'?"

James Appleton pointed across the car at Mary. "I was not speaking to you," he said.

Uh-oh, thought Detective Evans. *Big* mistake.

Mary marched around the car and seized Appleton by the collar of his jacket with both of her hands. "Did . . . you . . . say . . . 'kids'?" she repeated slowly. Her voice was almost a growl.

Appleton cut his eyes toward the detective. "I suggest you answer her question," Evans said.

"I . . . uh . . . two k-kids," he stammered. "They came into my hotel, barred the door . . . and now the fire alarm. I just know it's them."

"Was there a girl?" Mary asked.

Appleton nodded. "Redhead."

Mary pushed the small man away and pointed at the detective. "I'm heading to the hotel," she said.

CHAPTER 32

7:43 p.m.
Saturday, December 16
G Street, Washington, DC

"We're here," the taxi driver announced as he brought the cab to a stop. Directly across the street was an old red-brick building that looked as if it had been squeezed into the narrow gap between the tall modern buildings on either side. The words STEAMING MONKEY COFFEE EMPORIUM were written in large white letters across the awning between the first and second floors. The tall windows on the front of the building glowed warmly. The snow seemed to be growing heavier by the minute.

Camille stepped out of the car.

"How much?" Art asked the driver.

"Twelve dollars," he answered. "And don't forget the tip."

Art handed him two twenty-dollar bills. "Keep the change," Art said. "And if anybody asks, you never saw us."

"Not my first rodeo," the driver said as he took the money. "Don't know ya, ain't seen ya."

Art took his backpack and stepped out of the cab. He

stood on the sidewalk next to Camille as the taxi pulled away.

"Anything?" she asked.

Art looked up and down the street for a trace of something familiar, but there was nothing. "Not yet."

They made their way across the street and up a narrow set of concrete stairs to the entrance to the coffee shop. They stood at the top of the steps as Art glanced around once again. The snow was making it difficult to see much more than fifty feet or so into the night—the boy felt as though he were in a snow globe. And nothing looked familiar. He closed his eyes. Art could hear music playing inside and the sounds of conversation. The air smelled thick of coffee. But the dam in his head remained firmly in place, the memories just out of reach.

"I'm cold," said Camille as she nudged the boy from behind.

Art opened his eyes. The Yankees cap on top of Camille's head was dusted with fresh snow. "Sorry," he said.

He opened the door and they stepped inside.

The coffeehouse was long and narrow with high brick walls, a rusted tin ceiling, and wide oak flooring. Small wooden tables filled with twenty-somethings lined the left side of the room, and a long coffee bar with a massive chrome espresso machine occupied the right side. Large copper pendant lights hung from the ceiling and bathed the room in a golden glow. An eclectic collection of paintings and photographs adorned the walls. Jazz—maybe Miles Davis—played in the background.

"Anything?" asked Camille.

Art shook his head. "No. Not yet."

Give it time, he told himself.

Camille prodded him. "Hungry?" she asked. She pointed to a glass cabinet filled with baked goods.

Art pulled a twenty-dollar bill from his pocket and handed it to Camille.

"Get us something to eat," he said. "I'm going to the rest-room."

Camille watched as Art headed toward the rear of the coffee shop. She waited until he was out of sight and then rushed over to the counter. A short, thin girl with purple hair stood behind the register taking orders. She had a tattoo of Yoda on her left shoulder and a stud in her nose.

"May I please borrow your phone?" Camille asked politely.

The girl with the purple hair plucked a portable phone from its base and handed it to Camille. "Have at it," she said.

Camille took the phone and quickly dialed her home number. She held her breath as the line started ringing. She debated what to do if her mother actually answered—hang up, or try to explain what had happened? The reason Camille had called home, and not her mother's cell phone, was that she wasn't sure she had the courage to actually speak with her mom—at least not yet. She knew her mom would be worried—but also really mad.

Camille held her breath and listened as the phone rang once, twice, three times, four times, and then five times. No answer. There was a pause and then a click. The next thing she heard was her own voice on the answering machine on the other end of the phone. Camille let out a sigh of relief.

"Hi," her voice on the machine said, "this is the Sullivan residence. We can't take your call right now, but if you'll leave a message at the beep, we'll call you right back. Ciao!"

There was a slight pause and then a beep.

"Mom," said Camille, "I just wanted to let you know I'm okay."

She tried to keep her voice cheerful. She didn't want her mother to worry.

"I'll be home soon," the girl continued. "Things are a little crazy, but I'm keeping an eye on Art like I promised."

She paused for a moment.

"I love you," she finally said, and then ended the call.

7:48 p.m.
Saturday, December 16
Townhouse apartment, Washington, DC

It had happened far quicker than he had expected.

The phone call had come in from a landline, which

—although surprising—made it all the easier to trace. The address instantly popped up on Palmer's screen—a coffee shop on G Street. The kids were moving fast—but where were they headed? The girl had called home and left a message. Palmer listened to the message. The boy was clearly up to something, but what?

How much does he remember? Dorchek Palmer wondered.

The boy and the girl had already incapacitated four members of his team—four of the toughest, most highly trained people on the planet had been rendered useless by two tweens.

Pure luck, Palmer kept trying to convince himself. Unfortunately, Palmer didn't believe in luck. The kids were smart and resourceful, and his team had underestimated them at every turn. Palmer knew he could no longer take anything for granted. The key to the entire operation—an operation that had been in the planning stages for years—now rested on finding a boy with amnesia who was wandering around Washington, DC. If they didn't find him, everything could fall apart. The consequences could be earthshattering. Palmer did not intend to find out just how earthshattering.

He called Nigel Stenhouse, his remaining team member. Stenhouse could be at the coffee shop in less than a half hour. Palmer's directions to Stenhouse were clear: Do anything necessary to retrieve the boy.

Anything.

CHAPTER 33

7:49 p.m.
Saturday, December 16
Hotel Monaco, Washington, DC

The boy and the girl did this?

Impressive.

Detective Evans stood in the lobby of the Hotel Monaco. The Christmas tree, which had apparently fallen on some poor guy, still covered half the floor. The guests in the lobby seemed oblivious to the perilous circumstances around them—if anything, they seemed to be enjoying the absurdity of the situation.

A hotel security officer had approached the detective and Mary Sullivan as soon as they had entered the hotel. The security officer had handed over Camille's distinctive red jacket with white polka dots. "Found this on the front steps," he had explained. "Several of the guests reported seeing a blond boy and red-haired girl running through the lobby and up the stairs. We were looking for them when the alarm went off."

"Where do the stairs lead?" Mary had asked.

"Conference rooms, meeting rooms, ballrooms," the security officer had replied. "But the kids seem to be long gone. No sign of them."

The security officer's explanation had not satisfied Mary, who immediately headed up the stairs in search of her daughter and her charge.

The detective now stood alone in the lobby with the security officer and pondered her next move. There was a question she needed to ask, but she was afraid she already knew the answer.

"I need to see the security footage," said the detective.

The officer paused. He seemed somewhat embarrassed. "Well," he finally said, "funny you should ask."

"It's been erased, hasn't it?" said the detective.

The security officer seemed surprised. "Every bit of it," he said. "Every camera, every angle, every monitor. All gone. Strange, huh?"

The detective nodded. "Very strange."

7:50 p.m.
Saturday, December 16
Steaming Monkey Coffee Emporium, Washington, DC

"You okay?" the girl with the purple hair asked.

Camille nodded. "I'm okay," she replied. "Just checking in with my mom—you know how parents can be."

The girl with the purple hair laughed. "Been there plenty of times," she said. "Parents worry." She extended her hand to Camille. "By the way, my name's Tricia."

Camille shook the girl's hand. "Camille," she said.

Tricia pointed behind Camille. "And is that your brother?"

Brother? Camille wondered. What's she talking about?

And then it hit her. The barista was talking about Art. Camille glanced over her shoulder. He was less than ten feet away.

Camille reached across the counter and managed to drop the phone back into its base just as Art approached. Although she didn't think calling home was such a big deal, she knew Art would freak if he caught her on the phone. He was way too paranoid.

"What'd you get?" Art asked as he made his way next to her.

Camille pretended that she had been reaching for one of the menus lying on the counter. "Haven't decided yet."

"Ready to order?" asked Tricia, as if on cue.

The espresso machine beside her hissed and steamed. A husky bearded man in a dark blue T-shirt stood in front of the chunky metal machine and churned out shot after shot of the dark coffee extract. On the front of his T-shirt—in large uppercase letters—was the word "BOB."

"I'll have an iced mocha," said Camille. "Medium. And a lemon bar."

It had been a couple of hours since they last ate, and she was famished.

"Bob—one iced mocha, medium," Tricia called to the man in the dark blue T-shirt. Bob merely grunted and continued tamping espresso grounds into a clean filter.

"And what can I get for you?" Tricia looked at Art.

Art opened his mouth to respond, then stopped and sniffed the air. He turned to Camille.

"Do you smell that?" he asked.

"Smell what?" asked Camille.

"He probably smells the wheat-grass white-mocha vegan brownies," said the girl with the purple hair. "They're our most popular item, but they have kind of a distinctive smell —they're made with mushrooms, so they can get a little funky. Bob makes them fresh every day. If you can get over the smell, they taste great."

Bob grunted his approval but never looked up from his coffee duties. Shots of espresso continued to flow unabated.

"No," said Art, "not that smell."

Art turned to a tall, lanky young man who had taken a position behind them in line. The young man wore a long-sleeve NYU T-shirt that was splattered with paint and a pair of brown pants. He looked as if he had not slept or showered for days.

Art sniffed the air deeply. He then pointed at the young man. "That smell," he said. "His smell."

Bob grunted his agreement from behind the espresso bar.

"Art!" Camille exclaimed in horror. "That's so rude."

"Can't blame the little guy for that," said the tall young man as he sniffed his right armpit. "I'm a bit gamy today — getting ready for a show next month, you know. Showers optional — but no judgments, okay?"

"Turpentine," said Art. "Am I right? You smell like turpentine."

The young man nodded. "I'm working on my master's degree in studio painting. I always smell like turpentine."

Art opened the front of his backpack and frantically felt around inside the pocket. His hand finally fell upon the object he was searching for and he pulled it out.

"There!" Art said triumphantly. He held out the small brass key engraved with the number 10. "Do you recognize this?" Art asked the student.

"How'd you get that?" the young man responded. He seemed genuinely surprised by the sudden appearance of the key.

"Do you recognize it?" Art asked again.

The student pulled a key chain from his pocket, selected a single key, and held it up for Art to see. It was virtually identical to the key Art had found in his backpack — the bow was even painted a brilliant blue. The only difference was the number engraved on the key — 12 instead of the number 10.

"It's a studio key," the young man said. "A lot of art students rent out studio space while we prepare for our shows.

Studio number ten is on the second floor—just down the hall from my studio."

"Studio?" asked Art. "Where?"

"Right down the alley from here," said Tricia, who'd been listening to the whole exchange. "It's an old manufacturing plant—or something like that. The main entrance is on the other side of the block, but there's a back entrance through the side alley."

Art didn't hesitate. He turned and headed out the door without another word.

Camille looked at Tricia. "I guess I'll get my mocha later," she said apologetically, and left the twenty-dollar bill on the counter.

Camille found the boy standing at the entrance to the alley. She was struck by how narrow the back street was. It looked as if she could stretch her arms out and touch both sides. And it was dark. The high brick walls on either side shielded out the light of the city, and the cool glow of the streetlight barely penetrated more than a few steps down the dark corridor. Even the snow seemed to be having a hard time making it into the thin space.

"Kinda dark," she said. "Maybe we should walk around the block to the front." She tried to hide the uncertainty in her voice. They had just been kidnapped from a museum, threatened with a stun gun, involved in a car crash, and chased through a hotel, barely escaping from the clutches of four thugs who clearly intended to capture them by any means necessary. Going down a dark alley did not seem like a great next step in their adventure.

"I'll go first," Art said calmly. "Stay close behind me."

He started walking forward, but Camille hesitated. Art turned and looked at her.

"Don't worry," he said. "There's light somewhere up ahead."

Camille nodded. She had no choice but to follow. Keeping an eye on Art was proving to be much more difficult than she had ever anticipated. She quickly caught up with him, and they stepped forward into the dark.

PART 3

"Even though one seeks with the expectation of finding, finding is a complete surprise nonetheless."
—letter from Vincent van Gogh to his brother Theo,
7 November 1881

CHAPTER 34

8:02 p.m.
Saturday, December 16
Downtown streets, Washington, DC

The cold night air had settled hard into the dark, narrow alleyway. Camille held firmly to Art's backpack and shuffled her feet to avoid tripping in the gloom. She listened intently for any sound that might signal the approach of pursuers. But the alley was disconcertingly quiet. The girl looked up. She could see the snow swirling in the sky far above her.

Glancing around Art's shoulder for any sign of light up ahead, Camille saw nothing. She had lost all sense of depth perception, and her inner GPS had failed her completely. How far had they walked? How far did they have to go?

"You okay?" asked Art.

"I'm fine," she replied, which was a complete lie. She was, in fact, exhausted, hungry, freezing, and scared.

"Just a little farther," he said. His voice echoed ever so slightly in the narrow canyon of brick and mortar. It occurred to Camille how much Art had changed since that morning. Quiet and uncertainty had given way to confidence and determination. She could hear the shift in his voice. She could see it in his eyes.

They shuffled forward slowly for a couple more minutes in the dark. Camille continued to listen for any sign that they were being followed, but the only sound she heard was the soft swish-swish of her feet as they made their way along the concrete path. The sound was soothing and rhythmic —it made her realize how tired she was. She thought of her soft, warm bed at home.

Suddenly, Art stopped. Caught off-guard, Camille stumbled forward and planted her face squarely into his backpack.

"Ouch!" she exclaimed.

"Shhh," Art whispered. "We're here."

He moved forward a couple of steps so she could see. Just a few yards to their right, a rusted lamp hung from the side of a windowless brick wall. Beneath its faint light was a metal door, painted a dingy gray and heavily dented. The kids made their way over to the entrance and stood beneath the lamp. Camille felt as if she were in a spotlight—not a particularly wonderful place to be, considering what they had already been through that afternoon.

There was a small sign on the door:

GEORGE WASHINGTON UNIVERSITY DEPARTMENT OF FINE ARTS

UNIVERSITY PERSONNEL AND STUDENTS ONLY

"Maybe you're some sort of genius," said Camille.

213

"Maybe you're already in college, and that's how you know so much about art."

"I'm not a genius," said Art.

Camille shrugged. "You never know."

Art grabbed the door handle, pushed down on the thumb lever, and pulled. The door didn't budge.

"Locked," he said. "Let's go around to the front of the building—maybe the door is open on the other side. Or maybe there's a window we can try to open."

"Or," replied Camille, "you could try the key."

It had clearly not occurred to Art that the studio key might also open the door into the building. He took the key from his pocket, placed it into the lock, and turned. Once more, he grabbed the door handle, pushed down on the thumb lever, and pulled.

The door opened easily.

"Then again," said Camille, "maybe you aren't a genius."

Art ignored her and peeked inside.

"Long hallway," he said to Camille. "But it looks empty."

He opened the door some more for Camille to step inside, removed the key, and followed her into the hallway. He pulled the door shut behind them and gave it a push to make sure it had locked.

The hallway was painted a pale industrial green—the sort of color you find in old hospitals and high schools—and the floor was a well-worn gray linoleum with little black specks. The building smelled of turpentine and dust. The

lights in the hallway—metal boxes filled with long fluorescent bulbs and built into the drop-down ceiling—were
spaced too far apart to properly illuminate the long, narrow
corridor, creating alternating pockets of deep shadows. To
their right was another metal door with a sign indicating
that it led to a set of stairs. The light from the illuminated
exit sign above their heads cast an eerie red glow around
them.

"Good thing there's nothing creepy about this place,"
said Camille.

Art pointed at the stairs. "Second floor," he said. "That's
where the guy at the coffee shop said we need to go."

"No," Camille replied. "He said the key goes to a room
on the second floor. He didn't say we had to go there."

But she knew there was no sense in arguing. Art had
already opened the door to the stairwell and stepped inside.
Camille reluctantly followed.

8:07 p.m.
Saturday, December 16
Hotel Monaco, Washington, DC

Detective Evans watched as Mary Sullivan made her way
down the stairs and across the lobby of the hotel. She could
see the disappointment in Mary's face.

Evans debated whether to tell Mary about the missing

215

security footage at the hotel. Earlier, when the detective had learned that the video at the National Gallery of Art had been erased, she had been willing to explain it away as a glitch in the system. But for security footage to disappear at two different locations was not a coincidence. It now seemed clear that whatever was going on involved way more than two kids wandering off from the museum.

"No sign of them," said Mary dejectedly as she made her way over to the detective. "And I looked. I mean, I really looked. In every room, under every table, in the stairwell. There's no way they're in this hotel."

"I've put out an alert for Camille and the boy," said Detective Evans. "There're going to be a lot of cops looking for those kids."

Mary nodded. She looked tired. "This has something to do with the boy, doesn't it?" she asked.

Detective Evans hesitated. "I don't think we can really know at this—"

Mary interrupted her. "The truth," she said. "Please."

"Yes," replied the detective. "I think this has something to do with the boy."

CHAPTER 35

8:09 p.m.
Saturday, December 16
GWU Department of Fine Arts studio building,
Washington, DC

Art poked his head out of the stairwell and surveyed the second-floor hallway.

"All clear," he said.

The two made their way down the corridor, past wooden doors with numbers stenciled in black paint. Tall transom windows capped each door.

Seven.

Eight.

Nine.

Ten.

Art stood in front of the door stenciled with the number 10. He paused, placed his ear against the door, and listened.

Nothing.

The boy stepped back and stared up at the large transom window above the door. The pane was completely dark. From all appearances, no one was in the room. But Art knew that appearances could be deceiving.

"Go ahead," Camille urged him. "Try the key."

He took the key from his pocket and then motioned for her to move away from the door.

"Seriously?" the girl asked.

"Seriously," the boy replied. "And if anything happens, don't stick around to ask questions. Just run."

"Nothing's going to happen," Camille insisted. "No one's in there."

"Promise me you'll run."

"I promise," she replied. She backed up to the opposite wall.

Art put the brass key into the lock, held his breath, and gave it a quarter turn to the right. The cylinder turned easily, and the bolt slid back with a slight click. The boy exhaled, removed the key from the lock, and returned it to his pocket.

"Well," he said, "I guess we're in the right place."

Art opened the door a crack. He paused once again and listened for any sounds from within. Again, all was silent.

He motioned for Camille to remain where she was. She rolled her eyes but stayed against the far wall in the hallway. Art stepped into the dark room.

Despite her bravado, Camille was scared. And contrary to what Art seemed to believe, she was not convinced that standing in the hallway was any safer than following him into the dark room. Every time she shifted her feet, the floor beneath her creaked. The sound seemed incredibly loud. If there was anyone in the building, they wouldn't be able to help but hear them.

Camille's eyes darted constantly from one end of the long hallway to the other.

Suddenly the lights in the room flickered on. Her heart jumped in her chest.

"Wow!" Art exclaimed from inside the room. His words echoed through the building. *So much for keeping quiet,* Camille thought.

"What is it?" she asked in a half whisper.

"Get in here!" Art said. "You've got to see this!"

8:10 p.m.
Saturday, December 16
Steaming Monkey Coffee Emporium, Washington, DC

"A young boy and a young girl," said Nigel Stenhouse. "The girl has red hair—bright red hair. The boy, blond."

The thin girl with the purple hair hesitated. She clearly did not like giving away information about a couple of kids to a complete stranger.

"Not sure," she said. "We get all sorts of customers— hard to keep up with them all."

Nigel Stenhouse nodded politely. The girl's response was not unexpected, but Stenhouse didn't have time to waste. He would need to put his secret weapon into action. Stenhouse was British, and he was about to unleash the full force of that English decorum against her.

He leaned over the counter.

"I understand your concern, miss," he assured her in his distinctive North London accent. His voice was almost a whisper. "But I'm not some nosy parker. The girl's name is Camille, and she's my niece. She called home just a few minutes ago, and her mum asked me to drop by and pick her up."

Stenhouse paused for effect.

"She's in a bit of trouble for staying out too late," he finally said. "Her mum's a worrier."

The girl with the purple hair immediately relaxed. Stenhouse knew that anytime he could squeeze the word "mum" into a sentence, it worked wonders. Americans loved to hear someone with an English accent say "mum."

"They left maybe ten minutes ago," the girl with the purple hair said. "The boy had a key to one of the art studios in the building behind the coffee shop. I think that's where they were headed."

An art studio! thought Stenhouse, who tried to hide his surprise. So maybe the boy wasn't simply wandering about the city at random. Maybe the boy had a plan—a destination. Palmer would want to know about this new development immediately. The pieces, it seemed, were starting to fall into place. And, it also seemed, their guest had been withholding information from them.

"Smashing!" said Stenhouse. "I truly, truly appreciate your help. Her mum will be ever so pleased."

The girl with the purple hair smiled warmly. "You're quite welcome."

CHAPTER 36

8:11 p.m.
Saturday, December 16
GWU Department of Fine Arts studio building,
Washington, DC

Camille gasped as she stepped through the doorway.

The room was massive—two stories tall, and long enough for a half-court game of basketball. The interior walls of the room were bare brick, and the floor was made of oak planks that looked as if they had been in place for a hundred years or more. Tall, narrow windows covered the far wall and steel I-beams crossed in the space high above their heads. A row of broad metal pendant lights hung near the ceiling along the length of the room. The lights were attached to an ancient collection of pulleys and chains that wound their way across the ceiling and down to a panel of brass hand cranks and levers beneath the windows on the far wall. The lights and the girders cast deep shadows throughout the room. The only sound was a slight hiss emanating from the ornate cast-iron radiator that ran down the left side of the room.

"Creepy," said Camille. "But really cool."

Art made his way over to the panel of cranks and levers along the wall. He selected a crank in the middle of the panel and held it tightly. With his free hand, he released the lever. He instantly felt the heft of one of the heavy pendant lights tugging against the crank. As he allowed the weight of the light to slowly turn the reel in a counterclockwise direction, one of the massive pendants in the middle of the room started to descend. Art stopped the light about fifteen feet or so from the floor and reset the lever. He then lowered two more lights. The deep shadows disappeared.

"Better?" asked Art.

"Better," replied Camille. She didn't bother asking how he knew how to operate the cranking system that lowered the lights. She didn't have to ask — she could see it in his eyes. The memories were returning — and fast.

The two stood and examined the room.

"It looks like . . . Dr. Frankenstein's lab," said Camille.

A thick wooden table ran through the middle of the room. On top of the table were Bunsen burners, beakers, burettes, tongs, funnels, scalpels, latex gloves, cotton swabs, tubing, clamps, bulbs, and test tubes. A computer keyboard and a huge microscope sat at the far end of the table next to a towering stack of notebooks and the largest computer screen Camille had ever seen in her life. On the opposite side of the table was a tall wire shelf filled with small containers made of a dark glass.

The girl made her way over to the shelf and looked at a label on one of the glass containers.

A look of horror crossed her face.

"Dragon's blood!" she exclaimed. "The label says it's dragon's blood."

What is this place? she wondered.

And why *does* Art have a key to it?

Art smiled. It may have looked like Dr. Frankenstein's lab to Camille, but it felt like home to him. He could sense the memories bubbling up. He was starting to feel like a real person.

"Dragon's blood," he said. "Sanguis Draconis. It's a red pigment made from a tree in Asia."

"A pigment?" asked Camille. "For what? It sounds like something out of Harry Potter."

"Painters have used stuff like that for centuries to make paints," he explained. "They would grind the pigment up and mix it with oil. Dragon's blood makes a great red paint. There's even a mural in Pompeii that has dragon's blood paint on it—and that's about two thousand years old."

Art stepped over to the shelf.

He read several of the labels aloud—boiled oil, hydrochloric acid, zinc oxide, ink of cuttlefish, ground mollusk shells, realgar, dragon's blood, powdered mummy, potassium chlorate, lapis lazuli.

"Art supplies," said Art.

"Not like any art supplies I've ever seen," said Camille. "Powdered mummy? You have to be kidding me."

Art knew they weren't like any art supplies that Camille —or most people—had ever seen. They weren't nice pre-packaged tubes of paint with pretty labels. They weren't paintbrushes made of some industrially manufactured bristles. They weren't convenient, easy-to-use aerosol cans filled with lacquer, or the nice premade canvases that you can buy in multipacks at the local craft store. No, the bottles on the shelf represented raw materials used by artists for centuries. Many of the items in the bottles were dangerous—poisonous, corrosive, and, if handled improperly, potentially explosive. Artists throughout the ages had sacrificed their health, and many their lives, by using these types of chemicals, minerals, powders, and liquids to produce their art. The boy knew that some people believed that van Gogh may have suffered from lead poisoning—a common ingredient in paints in the nineteenth century. But Art also knew that these same materials, as dangerous as they may have been, were also used to create many of the greatest works of art known to history.

8:12 p.m.
Saturday, December 16
Hotel Monaco, Washington, DC

Detective Evans and Mary Sullivan stood outside the front

entrance of the hotel. The night was cold, and the snow was growing heavy. The National Portrait Gallery, barely a hundred feet from the entrance to the hotel, was little more than a fuzzy blur. The traffic outside the hotel seemed remarkably light—perhaps everyone knew that even heavier snow was on the way.

"What now?" Mary asked.

"We keep looking," replied the detective. "And I need you to check with Camille's friends and any family you may have in the area—anyone Camille might go to if she was in trouble or needed help."

Mary nodded. She suspected that the detective was just providing her with busywork—something to keep her mind off the fact that her daughter was still missing. But that was fine—Mary needed the distraction. She had started making a mental list of whom she needed to call when her phone rang. She pulled her cell out of her purse—it was a call from her sister. Mary's heart jumped in her chest. She had forgotten that her sister had been heading over to her house. Maybe Camille was already there. Maybe her daughter was already safe at home.

"It's my sister," Mary said to Detective Evans as she answered the phone.

Brooke Evans had been a detective for ten years. However, she didn't need years of experience to read the look on Mary Sullivan's face.

She watched as the hopeful expression on Mary's countenance gave way to concern.

"Let me know if you hear anything else," Mary said before ending the call.

The worried mother stood at the top of the stairs outside the entrance to the Hotel Monaco and simply stared out into the cold, snowy night. The detective knew better than to try to push her to speak. Mary would talk soon enough.

And she did.

"There were two messages on our phone at home," she finally said. "The first message was from a Detective Wasberger."

"Wasberger?" asked Detective Evans. How did he get involved in all of this?

Mary continued to stare out into the night. "He said that Art's brother had shown up at the station looking for him — except he said the boy's name isn't Art. It's Taylor, and he's supposedly from Virginia. Detective Wasberger said the boy ran away from home. He gave the brother my address and phone number so he could call me and make arrangements to pick up Art . . . or whatever his name is."

"But the brother never called, did he?" asked Detective Evans. She knew Wasberger had just been trying to be helpful — but providing Mary's address and phone number had been a big mistake.

Mary shook her head. "No. He never called."

"And the second message?"

"From Camille," replied Mary.

"Your daughter called?" asked the detective. "What did she say?"

"She said things were a little crazy but that she was keeping an eye on Art like she had promised."

The detective did not immediately respond. *Things were a little crazy?* Whatever Camille meant by that, it didn't sound good. Mary, Evans could tell, understood that as well.

"Did she say anything else?" the detective finally asked.

"Just that she . . . would be home soon," said Mary. And with that, she burst into tears.

8:20 p.m.
Saturday, December 16
Townhouse apartment, Washington, DC

"Front entrance, one rear exit," said Dorchek Palmer. "No alarm system. Twelve studios, one stairway in the rear of the building, and an elevator near the main entrance. There's nowhere to run or hide once they go inside one of the studios—the rooms are long but narrow. Security camera on the front of the building, but I'm running an empty loop on that, so you're good to go."

Palmer had pulled up the floor plan for the building from a directory on the university's website. Nigel Stenhouse, the only remaining member of the team, sat in his vehicle—yet another large black SUV—and listened intently as Palmer spoke. Stenhouse understood the gravity of the situation.

"You'll have to go in alone," said Palmer. "Everyone else is out of commission. Do anything you need to do to finish the mission."

Palmer paused.

"No one," he finally said, "gets in or out of the building until we find that boy. Understood?"

"Understood," said Stenhouse.

"And one more thing," Palmer said.

"What's that?"

"Do not underestimate these kids."

8:21 p.m.
Saturday, December 16
GWU Department of Fine Arts studio building,
Washington, DC

"These are seriously art supplies?" said Camille, after spending several minutes inspecting the containers on the shelf. "What *is* this place?"

Art didn't respond. He went over to the computer keyboard and pushed one of the buttons. The large screen immediately lit up. Camille made her way over and examined the monitor. The panel itself was the thinnest and largest she had ever seen. The screen was at least four feet high and six feet wide. But what was more remarkable was the image on the monitor: a small text box against a brilliant blue background. The text box seemed to float in space — it looked remarkably lifelike, or as lifelike as a floating text box could be. The image was three-dimensional, but with a clarity Camille had never seen.

"You need a password," she said, stating the obvious.

Art stared down at the keyboard. A moment later he typed five letters.

"What did you type in?" she asked.

"*Verum*," he replied. "It means 'truth' in Latin."

"And how do you know that's the password?"

"I just know," the boy replied, and pressed Enter.

The small text box blinked out of existence, and an instant later another image appeared.

Camille gasped.

She stared at the picture on the massive computer screen. It was an image with which she was familiar — but not one she would ever have expected to see in this setting.

What have I gotten myself into? she thought.

CHAPTER 37

"Is that what I think it is?" Camille asked.

"Yes," replied Art.

They stared at the image floating on the screen. It was the long-lost painting by Vincent van Gogh, *The Park at Arles with the Entrance Seen Through the Trees* — the same painting that they had seen earlier that day on the large banners hanging from the front of the National Gallery of Art.

The image on the screen was remarkable.

"It's so . . . real-looking," said Camille.

Art nodded. It was incredible. He stood directly in front of the monitor, his face only inches away, but it was as if he were standing in front of the painting itself. There was no sense of the image being anything less than a real object — the boy could almost smell the dust in the intricate carvings on the thick wood frame. Whatever technology was used to capture this image was not something bought off the shelf at the local electronics store.

Art reached out and touched the painting on the screen. Instantly a small circle appeared and the area that he had touched was enlarged tenfold. The detail was unbelievable. The boy could actually see a single hair from a paintbrush trapped in the dried paint. He put his hands on either side of the circle and moved them apart. The circle expanded —and the image within enlarged even more. He could now see thousands of hairline cracks crisscrossing the surface of the painting.

Art touched the circle again, and it disappeared.

"Wow," said Camille. "But why is this here? Why would someone need this?"

Art continued to stare at the screen. "Good questions," he replied. He could feel the answers struggling to get out from behind the dam in his head.

"What else can you do with it?" Camille asked.

Another good question. "Let's see," the boy replied.

Art put both his hands under the bottom of the frame and moved them up. The painting shifted up, as if Art was actually lifting it. He brought his hands back down, and the painting settled into place. He then took the canvas by its right edge and moved his hand to the left. The painting rotated sideways. The edge of the frame appeared. He could see the little dings along the frame's perimeter and the small worn areas where the darkened wood peeked through

the gold paint—the hallmarks of the frame's many jour-
neys. Art turned the painting completely sideways. All he
could see was the edge of the frame itself.

Why would someone need to see the sides of a frame?
he wondered.

Art gave the frame one last push to the left, and the
painting rotated completely around on the screen so that
the back of the canvas was visible to them.

"No way," Camille said. "Is that . . . ?"

Art was at a loss for words. He immediately reached for
his backpack and retrieved the leather journal from its hiding place. He opened it to the tabbed page and held out the
drawing so that both of them could see it.

The back of the painting on the monitor—the verso—
was identical to the verso image in the journal. The spider
had made its appearance once again.

"Art?" Camille asked. "What does this mean?"

He did not immediately respond, but the pieces fell
together instantly—the leather journal, the newly discovered van Gogh at the National Gallery of Art, their mysteri-
ous pursuers, the strange room in which they now stood,
and the image floating on the screen in front of them.

He turned to Camille.

"The National Gallery of Art," the boy said, "is about to
pay one hundred and eighty-three million dollars for a fake
painting."

CHAPTER 38

8:30 p.m.
Saturday, December 16
GWU Department of Fine Arts studio building,
Washington, DC

"A fake painting!" Camille exclaimed. "But how? Why?"

Art held up the journal. "This is how," he said. "There are tons of old paintings by artists who never became famous. Art forgers buy those paintings from art dealers and use the old canvases when they fake a painting."

He pointed to the drawing in the journal. "According to the journal, this artist—Guillou—painted at the same time as van Gogh. They would have used the same kinds of art supplies—the same paints, the same brushes, the same types of canvases. The fake van Gogh was painted on Guillou's canvas, the one with the girl and her basket on the front and the spider on the back."

"So someone just painted a van Gogh painting over the picture of the girl?" Camille asked. "It can't be that easy, can it?"

"No," replied Art. "It's a lot more complicated than that. The canvas is just the start. You have to get rid of the old painting or it will show up on x-rays. Sometimes a forger will sand off the old painting or strip it off with chemicals. And then you have to make sure you use the right materials when you actually paint the new picture—oil paints that would have been around back then, nothing modern. Heck, sometimes forgers will even buy old brushes and use them."

Camille paused.

"Is that why these people are after us?" she finally asked. "They want the journal?"

Art nodded. "The spider proves that the so-called van Gogh canvas was not really used by van Gogh—it was originally used for another painting, Guillou's. It's probably the only proof that the long-lost van Gogh at the National Gallery is a fake."

"Wow," said Camille. She started to ask another question and then paused. She turned and looked around the room.

"What's the matter?" Art asked.

"It's sorta strange, isn't it?" she finally said.

"What's strange?"

"That you have a key to this room," she said. "And that you also have the only clue that could prove the painting's a fake."

"What do you mean?" asked Art.

"Think about it," the girl said. "This room's filled with art supplies that would have been used back when van Gogh was alive—you said so yourself."

Art nodded. She was right, but he didn't like where the conversation was headed.

"And how would you have gotten that journal?" she asked. "You said it probably came from an art collector or an art dealer, right?"

Art didn't respond.

Camille swallowed. "How do you know so much about art and how to fake a painting? We painted flowers in art class with paint that came in little plastic bottles—we didn't learn how to grind up mummies for paint. How do you know all that stuff? What if . . . and I'm just saying . . . but what if you have something to do with the fake painting?"

Camille was right. *How does a twelve-year-old boy know so much about art?* Art didn't have an explanation—it was all just there, in his head.

"I'm not an art forger!" he insisted. "I'm just a kid."

"I know you're just a kid," Camille replied. "But remember when you were telling me and my mom about seeing the Monet painting on my mug?"

"Yes."

"You had been with someone, right?"

"Yes."

"A man."

"Yes."

"What if that man is the art forger?" Camille suggested. "Maybe you're his son — or brother, or nephew, or whatever — I don't know. But what if the men at the museum really were police officers? What if the people at the hotel were police officers also? What if they are trying to get the journal to prove the painting is a fake?"

What Camille was saying made sense. And something in Art's head told him that she was far closer to the truth than he could imagine — and that scared him. What if he really was part of a plan to sell a fake painting to the National Gallery of Art for millions and millions of dollars?

There was a long silence.

"Are you mad at me?" Camille asked.

Art shook his head. "No. You might be right. I need to know the truth."

"So what's next?"

"We keep looking," he replied.

"No matter where it leads?" she asked.

"No matter where it leads."

CHAPTER 39

"So where do we start?" asked Camille.

Art pointed at the screen. "It's a computer," he said. "We need to see what else is on it."

Camille made her way over to the keyboard. "Easy enough," she said as she pushed the Escape button.

The image of the fake van Gogh painting blinked out of existence. In its place appeared a normal-looking desktop screen—several app icons and assorted document and image files. The desktop photo, however, stopped the kids in their tracks: a tall man with blond hair standing next to a shaggy-haired and equally blond boy. The man's arm was around the boy's shoulder. They stood in front of the Eiffel Tower. They both had huge smiles on their faces.

The boy in the photograph was Art.

He stared at the image on the computer screen.

In that instant, the dam broke.

The memories, all of them, flooded his head—and the boy remembered everything. It was as if a light had been turned on in a dark room. There was no transition. One moment the boy was an empty shell, and the next moment he was there—a full person.

 He knew that the Yankees were his favorite baseball team, that he always rooted against the Jets football team, and that he loved playing soccer. He knew that his favorite movie was the original *Star Wars* and that he despised Jar Jar Binks. He had once lived in Paris and had spent an entire summer in Egypt. He spoke French fluently and could read some Latin and Italian. He loved red velvet cake and hamburgers and couldn't stand olives. He was right-handed, had taken piano lessons for years, and once had had a gerbil named Sir Murphy. He knew that his favorite artist was Vincent van Gogh and that he had a giant poster of van Gogh's painting *The Starry Night* above his bed.

And he remembered standing beside his father in front of a painting at a small museum in Paris—*Impression, Sunrise* by Claude Monet. It was the first time he had seen the painting in person, and it was spectacular. How could he have forgotten?

The boy remembered everything—and it was overwhelming.

"Art?" Camille asked. "The man in the picture. Is that . . . your dad?"

The boy couldn't find the words to answer. He couldn't take his eyes off the screen.

"Art?" the girl said again. "Are you okay? Do you remember anything?"

The words finally came. "I remember everything."

"The man?" asked Camille. "Is that . . . ?"

Art nodded. "My father," he said. "Arthur Hamilton Sr."

Suddenly, everything made sense — but the sudden rush of memories didn't make anything better.

"Senior!" exclaimed Camille excitedly. "So you're a junior — Arthur Hamilton Jr.! Now we're getting somewhere."

Camille paused. She could see that Art was still struggling to absorb all the new information, but she had to ask the next question. Art had said they needed to keep looking for the truth — no matter where it led them.

She took a deep breath. "Did your dad make the fake van Gogh?" she asked.

Art didn't respond. He continued to stare at the computer monitor.

The girl felt terrible, but she had no choice. "Did your dad make the fake van Gogh?" she asked again.

Art shook his head. "No."

Camille let out a deep sigh of relief.

"My father's an expert on art forgeries," Art explained.

"He had been asked by the National Gallery to verify that the van Gogh painting was real. We've been living in DC for the last couple of months while he worked at the museum. We have a small apartment in Georgetown, but its only a place to sleep. The real work was done in here. He ran all the tests he normally runs, and everything seemed fine. But my dad knew something was wrong with the painting. He never said that directly to me, but I could tell it just didn't feel right to him."

"That's great!" Camille exclaimed. "You have the proof that the painting is fake. Now all we need to do is find your father and stop the museum from buying the fake painting."

"We can't find him," Art replied flatly.

"Why not?" said Camille.

"Because he's dead."

The room went silent.

Art stood in front of the computer screen as tears started rolling down his cheeks.

Camille tried to think of something—anything—to say. But what? Art had just told her that his father was dead. But for how long? And what did his death have to do with the fake van Gogh? Had the kids' pursuers killed him? She had so many questions, but one jumped out at her above all the rest.

"What about your mom?" she asked. "Maybe we could call her?"

Art wiped the tears from his face. "She died when I was

four," he replied softly. "It's just been me and my dad ever since."

Camille suddenly felt ill. She wanted to kick herself for asking the question about his mother.

"I'm sorry," she said. "I didn't mean to . . ."

"It's okay," he said. "That was a long time ago."

"But your dad?" Camille asked. "What happened? Did it have something to do with the painting?"

Art made his way over to the wire shelf and grabbed a small jar. He placed it on the table in front of Camille. The label on the container read COPPER ACETOARSENITE.

 "Van Gogh would sometimes use an oil paint called Emerald Green," he said. "The stuff in this bottle is what was used to make that paint. It's a beautiful color, but nobody uses Emerald Green anymore."

Camille bent down and examined the small brown canister. "Why not?"

"Because it's poisonous," said Art. "It's made of arsenic, and it'll kill you."

Camille jumped back from the jar. "Poison!" she exclaimed. "Why on earth would anyone use poison to make paints?"

"A lot of oil paints contained poisons back then," explained Art. "Sometimes they knew the stuff was poisonous, but the colors the poisons produced were great. Sometimes the artists just didn't know the stuff would kill them.

But that makes it easy to spot a fake — just check to see if the painting contains arsenic, lead, mercury, or all sorts of other poisonous stuff. If it doesn't, it's probably new — and a fake."

"But the long-lost van Gogh at the museum?" asked Camille.

"Filled with poisonous stuff," the boy replied. "And everything else checked out also. The canvas was old, the wooden stretchers were old. The painting has tiny little cracks all over it — just like an old painting would. And it passed the fingernail test."

"The fingernail test?"

"Van Gogh used oil paints," explained Art. "They're basically just a color and linseed oil, or some other oil, mixed together. Oil paints produce great colors and can be glopped on thick like van Gogh liked, but they take a long time — sometimes centuries — to dry completely. Artists use the same type of paints today. One way to tell if a painting is really old is to run the edge of your fingernail across it. If it leaves a mark, then you know it's not very old."

"But we know the van Gogh is fake," Camille said. "So how did the forger do all that stuff — the old paint, the cracks, the fingernail test?"

"You said this room looks like Frankenstein's lab, and you're right. It *is* a lab. There are thousands of people who could paint a perfect copy of a van Gogh — or a Rembrandt, da Vinci, or Renoir. That's actually the easy part. It's science that makes the painting look old — and it's science that finds the fakes."

Art pulled another jar off the shelf. "Potassium chlorate," he said. "Mix a little with hydrochloric acid and it will instantly rust a nail or a tack. And you can make wood look ancient with a mixture of vinegar and steel wool. You can literally take a brand-new frame and make it look hundreds of years old in less than an hour — but it leaves a chemical signal. The van Gogh didn't have any of the signs of a forgery — no unusual chemicals, no fake cracks, nothing."

"But if everything checked out, then why did your dad think something was wrong?"

"My father spent years looking at van Gogh paintings," Art said. "He just had the sense that something wasn't right. But he couldn't tell the National Gallery not to purchase the painting because of a hunch. He needed proof."

"And he got it," said Camille.

Art nodded and pointed to the large pile of papers, books, and ledgers on the far end of the table. "Records from auction houses and galleries from across Europe," he said. "My father collected them and read them constantly — the journal must have been one of those records. I remember sitting in this room — just a couple of days ago — when he got all excited. I remember that he was holding the journal, but he didn't tell me what was going on. It was late — around ten o'clock. He called this guy at the museum, the director of acquisitions. My father told him that they needed to meet right away. The next thing I know, we're headed over to the National Gallery. I fell asleep in the back seat on the way. I remember my father waking me up—we were parked in the underground garage at the museum. He told me to just keep sleeping—that he would be right back."

Art turned and looked out the window at the night sky. The snow swirled in the wind. His voice seemed distant and disconnected—as if he were on autopilot.

"I don't know how much later, but I remember him waking me up again. He told me to stay down and be quiet. He handed me my backpack and told me to hold on to it. He was whispering, which was strange—and that scared me. He told me that he would knock once on the back of the car. That would be the signal, he said. Once I heard that, I was supposed to count to twenty, get out of the car, and run toward the exit. He told me not to look back—just run. He didn't say why."

Art turned around and looked at Camille.

"It happened so fast," the boy said. "I had no idea what was going on. The next thing I remember is the knock on the back of the car. I was expecting it, but it still surprised me. I started counting. I heard a voice—a loud voice yelling at my father—but I kept counting. The voice seemed to move away. I could hear a big car engine. I kept counting. When I hit twenty, I opened the door, grabbed my backpack, and just started running as fast as I could toward the exit. And that's when I heard the gunshot."

Camille had no words. She wanted to tell the boy to stop. But she said nothing.

"He told me to keep running," Art continued. "He told me not to look back. But I did. I saw a man carrying my father over his shoulder. I could see blood on the side of my father's face. And he wasn't moving. The man threw him in the back of a . . ."

Art paused. He shook his head in disgust.

"They threw him in the back of a large black SUV," he said. "How could I have forgotten about the SUV? It was the same type of SUV that we were in when we were kidnapped from the museum. It was the same type of SUV as the one at the hotel."

The boy seemed once again to be on the verge of tears.

Camille could tell that Art was blaming himself for what had happened to his father. She needed to keep him talking.

"How did you get away?" she asked.

Art looked at her. He seemed to be processing the question.

"I ran," he finally replied. "I did what my dad told me to do. I ran up the exit ramp as fast as I could. They must have seen me. I could hear the SUV somewhere behind me. It seemed so loud. So close. I could see the lights coming around the turn in the ramp. I dove into these thick bushes along the driveway going into the garage. I kept crawling and pushing through the bushes. It was dark—I was trying to be as quiet as I could. I finally hit the outside wall of the museum, behind the bushes, and kept moving until I found a door. I tried to open it but it was locked. The voices —they were loud. They seemed so close. I just knew they were going to find me. I backed up against the wall—trying to hide—when I heard this beeping sound and the door clicked open. I got inside as fast as I could, shut the door, and just sat there. All I could think about was my dad—that he was gone."

"How did the door open?" asked Camille. "I don't understand—what happened?"

"I don't know," Art said. "The door was locked, so I don't know how . . ."

Art paused.

"Of course," he finally said.

"Of course?" said Camille. "What are you talking about?"

Art went over to his backpack and dumped the contents of the front pocket onto the table. Coins scattered and rolled all over. The boy reached down and grabbed something from the pile.

"This!" he said. He held up the small white plastic card they had found in the backpack.

"That?" said Camille. "Back at the museum you didn't even know what that was."

"I had amnesia," he replied. "Remember?"

"So what is it?" the girl asked.

"It's my father's keycard to the museum," the boy replied. "I must have backed into the keypad and accidentally activated the door."

Art held the card in his hand. "My dad put it in my backpack before . . ."

"Before he saved you," said Camille.

Art picked up the journal from the table and looked once again at the verso drawing. It was hard to believe that this water stain—shaped like a large spider—had caused so many problems. The journal, the boy had realized, was the only evidence that the van Gogh painting was a fake. Without the journal there was no way to prove that the canvas on which the fake van Gogh had been painted was the same canvas once used by a little-known French artist who happened to live at the same time as Vincent van Gogh. It was clear that several people wanted the journal destroyed —one hundred and eighty-three million dollars was a ton of money. Art knew that those people would do anything to destroy the journal. And if that happened, those people would win. His father's death would be meaningless. Art would not let that happen.

"We need to call the police," said Art.

"I thought you didn't trust anyone," said Camille.

"I told you that I trusted you," he replied. "And your mother. And Detective Evans. Let's start there, okay? Maybe that'll be enough."

Camille smiled. "I can't wait to get home," she said excitedly.

"Unfortunately," said a voice from across the room, "that's not going to happen anytime soon."

A tall man in a dark gray coat stepped from the shadows and pointed a gun directly at the kids.

CHAPTER 40

8:45 p.m.
Saturday, December 16
GWU Department of Fine Arts studio building,
Washington, DC

Nigel Stenhouse could not believe his luck.

He had not only located the boy—he had actually found the spider itself.

Truth be told, it had not been difficult finding the boy and the girl in the large brick building. He had heard them stomping around upstairs as soon as he entered the front door. Getting into the large studio had also been a snap—picking the lock on a simple dead bolt had been child's play. He had slipped in silently and watched from the shadows.

"Don't try anything," said Stenhouse as he made his way over to the large table with the computer. He waved his gun in the air for emphasis. The boy and the girl instinctively backed up against the wall. With his free hand, Stenhouse reached into his coat pocket and retrieved a small flash drive, which he inserted into a USB port on the computer.

The processor started humming immediately. In a matter of seconds, the flash drive would forward every file on the computer to Dorchek Palmer. Once that action was complete, the flash drive would destroy the computer's hard drive and every bit of data on it.

But while that process was under way, Stenhouse had other business to attend to. He pointed his gun at the boy, who stood on the far side of the table in front of the massive windows. "Hand over the journal," Stenhouse said firmly.

The boy didn't move.

"Hand over the journal," repeated Stenhouse.

The girl, who stood next to the boy, looked over at her friend. She was clearly scared. "Give it to him, Art," said the girl. "It's not worth it."

The boy still didn't move. Stenhouse could hear the computer humming louder and louder. The destruct phase was almost complete.

"Listen to the girl," said Stenhouse. "Give me the journal, and everything will be fine."

The girl placed her hand on the boy's shoulder. "Please give it to him," she implored. "I just want to go home."

The boy finally spoke. "They're never going to let us go home."

Camille stared up at Art in disbelief. A moment ago they were preparing to call the police—she would have been back home within the hour. And now? Now she had a large man pointing a gun at her. And if Art was right, she was never going to make it home.

"What do you mean, they're not going to let us go home?"

Art never took his eyes off the man. "He can't let us go," the boy said. His voice was calm and flat, which actually scared Camille more than if he had been showing some sort of emotion. "He's destroying any evidence this journal ever existed. Do you hear the computer? It's overheating. This guy's destroying all the files. And even if he gets this journal too, that wouldn't be enough. Do you think the National Gallery will pay a hundred and eighty-three million dollars for a painting if there's any possibility it's fake? Not a chance—so he has to get rid of everything."

It took a moment for Camille to process what Art was saying. But when she did, she felt as though she had been punched in the gut. "He has to get rid of us," she said. "We're 'everything.'"

Art nodded. "Just like they got rid of my dad."

The man across the table smiled, which Camille found very creepy under the circumstances. "Bravo," the man said. "You're just like your dad—too smart for your own good. You've figured everything out—the fake painting, the spider, everything. But you've got one thing wrong—your dad's not dead. At least not yet."

* * *

Sometimes the world moves fast. It flies by in a blur. Hours seem like minutes, and minutes seem like seconds.

At other times—rare times—the clock almost stands still. Events unfold in slow motion. This was one of those times.

The words from the man with the gun seemed to hover in the air.

"Your . . . dad's . . . not . . . dead."

The words echoed in Art's head.

The boy's mind fought to make sense of the words. Maybe it was a trick. He struggled to reconcile what the man had just said with what Art had seen two days ago in an underground parking garage at the National Gallery of Art.

"My dad?" the boy said. "He's alive?"

Art's calm demeanor was gone in an instant.

"Yes," said the man. "And if you cooperate, maybe he'll stay that way."

That had to be a lie. The people who had pursued them all day were about to commit the greatest art crime of all time—how could they leave any witnesses around? Art glanced down at Camille. Her eyes were ringed with red—she seemed on the verge of tears. He knew she was exhausted. It was time to end this.

"Your dad," she said, "he's still alive!" Her voice was quivering. A desperate hope hung in her words.

Art nodded. Maybe the man was telling the truth. Maybe. Or maybe it was just another lie in a day full of lies.

But if there was a chance—even just a small chance—that his father was alive, then the boy had to find out.

Art looked down at the leather journal in his hand. It was the key to finding out whether his father was alive or not.

The boy stepped forward and dropped the journal onto the middle of the table. He then resumed his place against the wall next to Camille. His back pressed hard into the panel of cranks, levers, and gears that controlled the lights in the room.

"Smart boy," the man said. "Now just stay where you are and don't do anything stupid."

Art never took his eyes off the man. He put his left arm around Camille's shoulder. "It'll be okay," he said. "You'll see."

"Very touching," the man said as he bent over to retrieve the journal from the table.

The metal click was the first peculiar thing he noticed. It had come from the direction of the boy.

It's hard to say what happened next. All Stenhouse could remember was that it happened fast. There had been no time to react.

There had been the sudden smile on the boy's face— more of a smirk, really. Stenhouse should have shot the kid right then and there.

He remembered that the girl's head snapped up toward the ceiling—the briefest hint of a smile starting to form on her face.

And there was also the sudden change in light—the intensity increased rapidly. It was as if Stenhouse had a spotlight on him.

Or perhaps it had been the whirring sound above him.

Stenhouse didn't have time to process what was going on—he just knew it was going to be bad.

And it was.

Art had put his arm over the girl's shoulder. Camille thought he had done this to comfort her. But as soon as the man had reached across the table to retrieve the journal, the girl had felt Art's hand lift from her shoulder. There had been a flash of movement to her left and then a metal click.

It took a moment for Camille to realize what was going on. But when she did, she smiled—Art had released the lever on the light directly above the table.

Everything happened so fast after that.

The huge metal pendant lamp dropped like a stone. The sound of steel cables zipping through ancient pulleys filled the room. The light hit the man flush on his right shoulder, and his gun dropped to the floor. The man staggered back. Camille saw a look of surprise and then anger flash across the man's face.

There was another click, and another, and another. Art was releasing the lights as quickly as he could.

The man stepped to his left and avoided a lamp that came to a stop just three feet from the floor. He looked up in triumph, but the victory was short-lived. The next light hit him directly on top of his head. The man dropped immediately to the floor. The clang echoed throughout the room.

"Wow," Camille said. *Wow. Maybe we would go home, after all.*

Art ran over to the metal shelf and started rummaging through a plastic storage container. The bin was labeled OFFICE SUPPLIES.

"It's in here somewhere," he said. "Dad always kept some around."

"Kept what?" Camille asked. "What are you looking for?"

"This!" Art exclaimed. He pulled a silver circular object from deep within the box and held it out for her to see.

"Duct tape?" the girl asked.

"You can do anything with duct tape," said Art.

He made his way around the table to where the man lay on the floor. He could see that a giant red goose egg was already forming on the man's forehead.

"Help me turn him over," said Art.

"Why?" asked Camille. "We need to get out of here. There might be more of them nearby."

"Trust me," said Art. "Now quick, before he wakes up."

Art grabbed the man by one arm and pulled. Once the boy had the man's shoulder off the ground, Camille bent down and pushed. The man tumbled over on his stomach. The side of his face hit the wood floor with a thunk.

Art took the man's arms and pulled them behind his back. The boy bound the man's wrists, hands, and forearms together with the thick silver tape. Seconds later, the man's ankles and shins were also bound together. Art then lifted the man's face ever so slightly and put a short piece of duct tape across his mouth.

"He won't be going anywhere soon," Art said.

Camille agreed. The man was basically a duct tape mummy. Even with a lot of help and a sharp knife, it would likely take a half hour to free him. Art reached inside the man's jacket and pulled out his cell phone. He then retrieved the journal from the table.

"So now we call the police?" asked Camille. "We've got one of the bad guys—and the journal."

"Change of plans," said Art. There was no longer any uncertainty in his voice; he was no longer a blank slate. Camille could see that he knew exactly who he was, why he was there, and what he was supposed to do.

"What do you mean, 'change of plans'?" she asked nervously. "We've done everything we can do."

"Not everything," said Art. "Now I've got to save my dad."

CHAPTER 41

9:07 p.m.
Saturday, December 16
Downtown streets, Washington, DC

Art pressed the folded-up piece of paper into Camille's hand. "Promise me," he said.

Camille nodded as she stuffed the paper deep in her pocket. "I promise."

"I have to do this," he said. "I have to do it my way."

"I know," she said

She wanted to cry, but she held back the tears. He didn't need to see her cry. He needed to believe in what he was going to do. Camille wondered whether she would ever see him again, but she kept those doubts to herself. The quiet boy she had met the night before no longer existed. Art was now Art—focused, intense, and incredibly determined.

The boy stepped out of the shadows of the alleyway and into the heavy snow that was falling. He glanced up and down the street while putting on the gloves from his backpack—Camille still wore his blue jacket—and then looked back at her.

"Wait five minutes," he said.

Camille didn't respond. A moment later Art disappeared into the thick white cover of the snow.

The temperature hovered just above zero, and the snow was dropping in thick sheets. It was the wind, however, that was truly brutal. It roared down the street and straight into his face. It didn't matter which way the boy turned or which street he took, the wind always seemed to find him. His eyes watered, and his cheeks burned. Art could feel his jaw growing sore as the cold set in, deep in his head. He couldn't bury his hands far enough into his jeans pockets. His whole body felt stiff and unnatural. The shoulder he had injured in the car wreck throbbed in pain. But none of that mattered. Although he had plenty of money for a cab, he had made the decision to walk. He wanted to be out in the cold.

Art had taken this walk before—with his father. After two days of not knowing his own name and not remembering anything about who he was, the boy now clung fiercely to every memory. Since his mother's death, Art had spent almost every waking moment with his father. Art didn't have any friends to speak of—he was never in one place long enough to really get to know anyone. Instead, he had traveled the world with his father, going from city to city and museum to museum. He had probably spent more time around great works of art than any other twelve-year-old on the planet. Art had seen things and visited places very few kids his age ever got to see — all thanks to his father.

It seemed strange, but the boy finally understood why his mind had shut down for the past two days. The doctor at the hospital had called it dissociative amnesia — a loss of memory from a traumatic event, to put it simply. Believing his father had died and then barely escaping with his own life probably fit the description of a "traumatic event." Art now understood that his mind had simply been protecting him — his father was all he had.

The boy was still putting together some of the missing pieces from the past couple of days, and the hours following his father's disappearance remained fuzzy. He vaguely remembered waking up in a maintenance closet at the museum. He had a faint memory of taking his backpack to the coat check and leaving it there. He remembered making his way to the room where he was found by the docent — a room filled with paintings by Vincent van Gogh. It was as if something deep inside of him had been pushing him along — guiding him down a path he was now determined to follow.

Ignoring the wind, he made his way down Seventeenth Street and past the Old Executive Office Building. President Harry Truman, his father had once explained, despised the building — Truman thought it was ugly. Art thought the structure was beautiful and majestic, particularly at night.

Continuing down Seventeenth Street, the boy passed the impressive stone façades of the buildings occupied by the Red Cross, the Daughters of the American Revolution, and the Organization of American States, all lit up beautifully. He continued south to Constitution Avenue and took a left. Directly across the street stood the Washington Monument, barely visible behind the thick wall of falling snow. Despite the cold, Art lingered there for a moment.

And that's when the phone in his pocket started ringing.

It was about time.

Art slipped off a glove, removed the phone, and pushed the button on the screen. Someone started speaking before the boy had a chance to say anything.

"You were supposed to report in," a voice said. "You're late."

The voice was much younger-sounding than Art had expected.

"I'll make you a deal," Art said.

There was silence on the other end of the phone. Art was tempted to say something else, but he knew he had to be patient. Even though his bare hand was freezing, he had to stick to his plan.

"I don't make deals," the voice finally said.

Art ignored that assertion. "My father for the journal. That's the deal."

Again there was silence.

"I don't make deals," the voice repeated.

Art knew the person on the other end of the phone was bluffing.

"You don't have a choice," Art said.

Silence.

Art had him.

"You have a deal," the voice finally responded. "When? Where?"

"The Pantheon," replied Art. "At exactly midnight. And if my father isn't with you, I'll know."

"The Pantheon?" said the voice. "What are you talking about?"

Art ended the call, and the line went dead. He removed the battery from the phone and dumped both the device and battery in a nearby trash can. His hand was shaking from the cold as he slipped his glove back on. Pulling the Sullivans' thick sweater tightly around him, the boy buried his hands in his pockets again and headed down Constitution Avenue toward his destination.

9:13 p.m.
Saturday, December 16
Starbucks, Washington, DC

Officer Pat McCarthy took his time preparing his coffee.

A little sugar.

A little cream.

Stir.

Sip.

Repeat until perfect.

He had time to get his coffee just right. With the exception of the incident at the Hotel Monaco, it had been a quiet night in his part of the city.

McCarthy took another sip.

Perfect.

He fixed the lid on his cup and was headed for the door when he remembered the other reason he had stopped in at the Starbucks on Fifteenth Street. He made his way back to the counter. A thin young man with a nametag that read RICK stood behind the register.

"Can I get you something else?" asked Rick.

"Nah," said the officer. "Just forgot to ask something. We have an alert out for a couple of missing kids. One's a boy, age twelve or so, blond hair. The other's a girl, ten years old, with bright red hair. Seen anyone matching those descriptions tonight?"

"You're kidding me, right?" asked Rick.

"Listen," said the officer. "Don't bust my chops over this —I gotta ask. Kids went missing from the National Gallery a few hours ago, so everyone's having a fit, particularly with the snow falling like it is."

Rick shook his head. "Not what I meant," he said. "Look behind you."

The officer turned around. Standing directly behind him was a girl who appeared to be around ten years of age, with bright red hair.

"My name's Camille Sullivan," the girl said. "And I want to go home."

CHAPTER 42

9:45 p.m.
Saturday, December 16
Storage closet, Washington, DC

Art opened the small closet and slipped inside. He turned on the light and pulled the door shut behind him. He could feel his entire body starting to slowly defrost. It had been a long walk, and despite the sweater and gloves, he still shivered from the cold. He sat down and rested for a moment in the small warm room.

Three years ago his father had been asked to examine a painting by Rembrandt that hung in the State Apartments at Windsor Castle just outside London. Art knew that questions always surrounded paintings attributed to Rembrandt. The royal family wanted his father's opinion—was it a real Rembrandt or not?

The State Apartments, located in the Upper Ward of the Windsor Castle complex, have served as a residence for the British Royal Family for centuries. One beautiful fall afternoon, after the crowds of tourists had departed, Art and his father had been escorted through the massive building by a kindly gentleman named Norris. The Rembrandt painting hung in a room overlooking a small stand of trees to the north of the castle. Norris had offered Art a brief tour of the building while his father examined the painting, a proposition that Art had immediately accepted. The tour, it turned out, was spectacular. Art particularly liked the suits of armor that seemed to be standing all over the place. Just as the tour was about to end, Norris stopped near a tall wooden archway and pointed at the thick wall that separated two rooms.

"There are secrets in these walls," the gentleman said, almost in a whisper.

"What kind of secrets?" Art asked.

Norris looked down at Art over his glasses. "Can I trust ye?" he asked.

"Yes," Art replied. "I promise."

Norris pondered Art's response and then, seemingly convinced, made his way over to the archway, which was paneled in oak that had aged to a deep reddish brown. Norris glanced around to make sure the two were alone, and then he pushed the bottom of a tall panel with his foot. There was a click and the panel popped open to reveal a secret passageway.

"Wow!" Art exclaimed. "And I just thought the walls were thick."

Norris smiled. "There are passages that run throughout the castle—hidden in the walls, floors, and staircases. Servants would use them to move about the household."

Norris carefully closed the panel, which blended seam-lessly back into the wall. "Remember," he had said, "there are secrets everywhere."

There are secrets everywhere.

It was a lesson that Art had learned well and applied often. After the visit to Windsor Castle, the boy had learned to ask for behind-the-scenes tours of the famous buildings and museums that his father visited in his work. The boy would ask to see any hidden passages, corridors, and rooms — places the public never went and never knew existed. The people in charge of these buildings always seemed more than willing to share their secrets — Art just had to ask.

Norris had been right — there were secrets every-where.

Art had packed a few supplies before leaving his father's studio. He carefully unloaded the contents of his backpack onto the floor of the closet. It was time to get to work. It was time for secrets.

9:47 p.m.
Saturday, December 16
First District Station, Metropolitan Police
Department, Washington, DC

Mary Sullivan could not stop hugging her daughter.

"I'm probably grounded for a really long time," mumbled

Camille from somewhere deep within her mother's smothering embrace.

"The rest of your life," replied Mary. "And then some."

Mary released Camille from the bear hug, stood back, and wiped the tears from her face. "Detective Evans has a few questions for you," she said. "And then we'll discuss what happened today."

Camille nodded. There was no sense in fighting the inevitable. But it wasn't the questions that bothered the girl — it was the answers. Camille took a seat in the chair next to the detective's desk. Her mother excused herself and left Camille alone with the detective.

"You had us worried tonight," said Detective Evans as soon as Mary was out of earshot.

"I'm sorry," Camille said. "I was just trying to help Art. I promised my mother that I would keep an eye on him."

"We're all trying to help him," said the detective. "That's why it's so important that you tell me everything that happened."

"I'll do my best," replied Camille, "but there's really not much to it. Art sort of freaked out at the museum after my mom went to the restroom. He took off down one of the hallways. He kept saying he had to get somewhere, but all we did was wander around the city. I'm not sure he knew what he was doing. I finally got tired and cold and told him I wanted to go home."

Camille knew her story was short on details and not even close to the truth—but it was the best she could do under the circumstances.

"Any idea where he might be headed?" asked the detective. "We still need to find him. It's really cold outside and the snow's getting heavier. We're all very worried about him."

"I'm worried about him too," replied Camille. "But he didn't tell me where he was going."

This was true. Art had a plan—but he did not tell Camille what it was. And she had not asked. Nor had she asked what was on the small, folded-up piece of paper that he had given her. The time for that would come soon enough.

"Think," said the detective. Her voice was calm and reassuring. "Was there anything he said that might help us find him?"

Camille paused and pretended to consider the question.

"Not that I can remember," she finally said. "I'm sorry."

This was a lie. Lightning was sure to strike the girl at any moment. There were lots of things that Art had said—and that Camille knew—that would blow the detective's mind. But the girl had made a promise to her friend.

The detective leaned over and put her hand on Camille's knee. She looked the girl directly in the eyes. "I want you to take some time and think about what happened," Evans said.

"It could be dangerous for him out there all alone. If you think of anything—*anything*—please let me know."

Camille looked directly back at the detective. She knew better than anyone how dangerous it could be for Art. "I'll let you know if I think of anything."

Evans sat back in her seat. Camille didn't think the detective was buying her story. But it didn't matter. A promise was a promise.

CHAPTER 43

It was only a short drive from his downtown apartment to the worn-down industrial building in the northeast section of Washington, DC, but he might as well have traveled to another planet. Things change fast inside the Beltway. The fantasy world of multimillion-dollar town homes and hyper-expensive office buildings quickly give way to the basic realities of urban life. The building on Third Street was as anonymous as they come—constructed of unadorned cinder block and surrounded by other plain cinder-block buildings with nothing to distinguish one from the other except the elaborate graffiti scrawled on the outside. But that's exactly what Dorchek Palmer had wanted when he purchased the former industrial site.

As he approached the building, a large steel security door slowly opened. Palmer's car pulled inside, and the steel door closed behind him with a clang. Lights flickered on inside the structure. Palmer stepped out of his car and looked around the large open space. There was some old industrial equipment piled in one corner and a couple of large trash cans filled to the brim with packing material in another. Otherwise, the building looked as if it had not been occupied for years.

Palmer made his way over to the stairwell at the rear of the building and stepped inside. A single light bulb hung from the first-floor ceiling. A rusty iron gate with a thick padlock blocked access to the stairs. Old newspapers and coffee cups were piled up behind the gate. In the back corner of the stairwell was a steel door with the fading words MAINTENANCE CLOSET barely legible on it. The door was rusted at the corners and appeared every bit as old as the building itself.

"Welcome back, Mr. Palmer," a voice said over a speaker.

Palmer nodded in the direction of a camera hidden in the corner of the stairwell.

With a buzzing sound, the steel door popped open. Inside the small closet was a dried-up string mop, an ancient bucket, and a cardboard box filled with empty tin cans. The small space still smelled faintly of industrial solvents and ammonia. Palmer stepped inside and pulled the door shut behind him. A moment later there was another buzz, and the rear of the closet opened up to reveal a shiny steel staircase. Palmer took the stairs down one floor to a room in the basement that would have fit in nicely with any of the modern office buildings just a few blocks to the south. Winston

Lantham sat at a desk watching a panel of monitors while Gleb Bazanov poured himself a cup of coffee. Both of them looked as if they had fallen out of a tall tree and hit every branch on the way down.

"How's our guest?" asked Palmer.

"Same as always," Lantham replied. "Quiet."

"I need to speak to him," said Palmer. He made his way over to a steel door at the end of the room. The door clicked open. Palmer stepped inside, and the door closed behind him. The room was well lit and constructed completely of concrete. Ventilation into the room was provided by way of several narrow shafts along the edge of the ceiling. The only furniture in the room was a small cot at the far end. A tall man — too tall for the small cot — was lying down on it, his legs splayed out over the end of the cot and his eyes closed.

"We have a bit of a problem, Dr. Hamilton," Palmer said.

"We have a problem?" asked the man lying on the cot. He kept his eyes closed.

Palmer did his best to maintain his composure, but his patience was worn thin. "I have a message from your son."

Hamilton remained flat on his back. "That's nice."

Palmer knew that Hamilton was not going to make this easy. He had refused to answer any questions about the whereabouts of the journal — or about anything, for that matter. Hamilton seemed to understand what was happening — and seemed remarkably unfazed by it all.

Palmer, however, suspected that he might now finally get the good doctor's attention.

"Your son has proposed a trade," said Palmer. "The journal for your freedom."

Arthur Hamilton Sr. remained poised, but it wasn't easy. Everything had happened so fast in the parking garage at the National Gallery of Art. After realizing far too late that Dr. Belette was part of the plan to sell the fake van Gogh to the museum, Hamilton had barely enough time to stuff the journal — and some money — into his son's bag. His last words to Art seemed ridiculous in retrospect — Hamilton had simply told his son to run and hide. But at the time that was the best he could do. He didn't know whom he could trust, and he just wanted his son to make it out of the parking garage alive. His son was smart — brilliant, actually. He knew that Art would eventually find his way to the police or the FBI — to someone who could help.

After the incident in the parking garage, the next thing Hamilton remembered was waking up in this room with a nasty headache — but at least he had still been alive. At that time, he had no idea what had happened to Art. Had he gotten away? The young man standing across the room — known to Hamilton only as Palmer — had served as Hamilton's sole contact with the outside world for the past day or so. Palmer had said nothing about Art. Hamilton took it as a good sign that the young man continued to pester him about the location of the journal. If they had located the journal, then they would have located Art. So if they didn't have the journal, that meant they didn't have Art—he was still out there somewhere. But how long could Art evade these people? Had he gone to the police, or was he on his own somewhere?

Hamilton had already rolled through all the possible scenarios of what could happen—and there were some pretty bad ones. He tried to stay positive, but it was difficult. Of all the situations he had considered, he had never expected that his son would try to strike a deal for his freedom—and that scared Hamilton, that Art was communicating directly with Palmer. But the arrangement also provided the only chance that he—and Art—might make it out of this mess alive. His son was up to something, but what?

There was only one thing he could do—trust his son.

Hamilton sat up and opened his eyes. "Go on."

"Your son has been quite the thorn in our side," said Palmer. "We've chased him across the city. He's sent two of my employees to the hospital, left one unconscious in an alley and another one unconscious in a hotel, and—quite frankly—I still haven't figured out what he's done to the last one I sent after him."

Hamilton smiled. Another surprise from his son. Apparently Hamilton had been raising Jason Bourne.

"So what's the deal?" asked Hamilton.

"That's just it," replied Palmer. "Your son didn't provide

a lot of details. The trade is supposed to take place at midnight tonight, but I'm not exactly sure where."

Hamilton had not had access to a watch or clock for . . . well, he wasn't sure how long. But the way his captor was talking, the time for the swap must have been getting close.

"What did my son say?" asked Hamilton.

"He said we would meet at the Pantheon," replied Palmer. "I have no idea what that means. Isn't there a Pantheon in Greece?"

The Pantheon.

Hamilton had to work hard to keep from laughing.

He knew exactly where his son intended to convene to exchange the journal for the hostage — and Hamilton also knew that his young captor was not going to be happy about it.

"Rome," Hamilton said. "The Pantheon in Rome, not the one in Greece. Most people think of the building in Greece, but that's actually the Parthenon."

The blood drained from his captor's face. "What?" he exclaimed. "Your son must be playing some sort of trick."

Hamilton shook his head. "Nope," he replied. "My son was talking about the Pantheon in Rome. That's where he wants to meet you tonight."

His captor stared across the room at the man on the cot. "We can't conceivably get to Rome by midnight. Neither can your son. It's not possible."

"It is possible," Hamilton said. *"Interior of the Pantheon, Rome* is a painting by a man named Giovanni Panini. He painted it in the early eighteenth century. It's quite lovely, I might add."

The painting showed the inside of the Pantheon, a Roman temple built in the early second century and a popular tourist destination. In the painting, tourists mill about in the spacious interior of the structure, under its grand dome. The painting was part of one of the children's tours at the National Gallery of Art. Hamilton had sat in front of this image with his son on several occasions and discussed the various people on display in the work of art. What was the lady in the bright blue dress saying to the lady in orange? Why were so many people kneeling? Art loved that painting.

"A painting," echoed Palmer.

"Yes," replied Hamilton. "And do you want to guess which museum it's hanging in right now?"

Hamilton's young captor did not respond. He simply turned and left the room without another word.

Hamilton smiled, lay back on the cot, and closed his eyes.

And so they were to go back to the National Gallery of Art.

This was, Dorchek Palmer realized, a chess match—and the boy had just made his move. Palmer had to concede that it was an unexpected and inspired move—like Bobby Fischer's sacrifice of his knight in his 1956 match with Donald

277

Byrne. And Palmer did not need to be reminded that Bobby Fischer, the greatest American chess player ever, had been only thirteen years old when he defeated Byrne, a leading American chess master at the time.

But Hamilton's son, as shrewd as he may have been, had made a serious miscalculation — he had elected to play a match on a chessboard over which Palmer had complete control.

The self-proclaimed grand master made the call to Dr. Belette and set his countermove in action.

CHAPTER 44

It was one of the first things he had noticed while walking around the National Gallery of Art this past week — massive, ornate iron grates on the walls in the main hallways and in many of the galleries. Art remembered thinking that the space behind the grates looked big enough for a man to crawl around comfortably. The layout reminded him of the hidden passageways at Windsor Castle — yet another secret waiting to be revealed. Late one afternoon, while waiting on his father to finish up for the day, Art had seen one of the museum's maintenance workers removing one of the grates in the East Sculpture Hall. The boy had immediately started asking questions. It turned out that the grates, and the spaces they covered, were part of the museum's ventilation system. The thick walls of the museum were, in many places, hollow. Depending on the season, either cool air or warm air circulated through the massive vents built into the very structure of the huge museum.

Art had also learned that there were several points in the museum where maintenance staff could enter the ventilation system to clean it out and remove the occasional mouse family that might make itself at home. One of those access points was near the west stair landing on the main floor. The door—barely four feet tall—was hidden in the back of a maintenance closet near the stairs leading to the ground floor. The entrance led to a ventilation shaft that ran down an interior wall of the museum and through several galleries —including Gallery 30, the area in which the painting of the Pantheon by Panini was located.

Art now sat inside that ventilation shaft—within the wall of Gallery 30. The painting of the Pantheon was on the opposite wall. The boy had no idea what time it was or exactly how long he had been sitting there. Warm air drifted slowly through the ventilation shaft. Art felt as if he could simply lie down and go to sleep—but sleep wasn't an option.

He knew what his father would have said. Arthur Sr. would have told him to call the police—protect himself, turn over the journal. But Art knew exactly what would happen then—the men who had been chasing the boy would disappear into the wind, and his father would never be seen again. Art wasn't going to let that happen.

And so he sat in the ventilation shaft and waited.

A few minutes later he heard footsteps echoing in the distance and the indistinct murmur of voices. He closed his eyes and listened for any sign of his father's voice. The footsteps stopped.

Maybe it was just a security guard.

Art held his breath. For what seemed like an eternity, there was only silence.

And then suddenly the voices returned—but this time far more distinct and clear.

They were close.

The footsteps started again.

From the boy's vantage point, hidden deep in the shadows of the ventilation shaft and behind the thick iron grate, he had a perfect view of the painting—and his little gift.

As if out of nowhere, a man suddenly appeared. Short and balding, he shuffled across the room and stood in front of the painting. Art recognized him as Dr. Belette, his father's primary contact at the museum.

"This one," Belette said.

Another man appeared—this one young and thin.

Still no sign of his father. The boy started to wonder whether his father was still alive.

The young man turned to Belette. "What does that mean?" he asked. He sounded angry.

Belette shrugged. "I have no idea," he replied. He sounded nervous—almost on the verge of tears.

The young man stood there for a second and simply stared at the painting.

"Get him over here," he finally said to someone standing on the far side of the room, outside of Art's view.

A moment later a tall blond man limped over and stood next to Belette. The tall man took one look at the painting and laughed.

Even if he had not seen the man, Art would have known the laugh.

It was his father, and he was still alive. Art's heart thumped in his chest. He was sure that everyone in the room could hear the sound resonating through the echoing chamber of the ventilation system. The boy took a deep breath and tried to calm himself. The plan was falling into place. He had done everything he could do—it was now up to Camille. Art slowly started sliding himself back down the dark ventilation chamber and away from Gallery 30.

"What's that supposed to mean?" demanded Dorchek Palmer.

Arthur Hamilton smiled at the small note taped to the bottom of the painting by Panini. It read simply: *"Le journal est avec le poète vertueux."*

"It's from my son," he said. "He wanted to make sure you brought me to the museum tonight."

"So it's a trick," said Palmer.

"No," said Hamilton. "It says exactly where the journal

can be found. But my son knew the note would be useless unless I was here to decipher it."

Hamilton suspected his son was watching or listening to him as he spoke—but where and how?

He continued. "The French means 'The journal is with the virtuous poet.'"

"The journal I understand," said Palmer. "But who is the poet?"

Hamilton smiled. "It's a reference," said Hamilton, "to another painting in this museum. I suspect that even Belette could have figured it out—given enough time."

"Now, wait a second," replied Belette. "I know the paintings in this museum better than—"

"Better than me?" interrupted Hamilton. "Then please feel free to explain what this means."

Belette remained silent. His face turned beet red.

"Enough games," said Palmer. "Explain."

"*Virtutem forma decorat*," said Hamilton. "That's Latin for 'beauty adorns virtue.' It was the poet's motto."

Belette gasped. "Leonardo!" he exclaimed.

"Leonardo?" asked Palmer. "Leonardo da Vinci?"

"Yes," replied Hamilton. "The journal rests with Leonardo da Vinci."

CHAPTER 45

12:00 a.m.
Sunday, December 17
First District Station, Metropolitan Police
Department, Washington, DC

Mary Sullivan sat in an empty office sipping a cup of coffee. Next to her, on a small couch, Camille was curled up, her eyes closed. Her daughter had insisted that she wasn't tired, but Camille had fallen asleep almost as soon as she had plopped down on the couch. Mary Sullivan decided to let her sleep. She could tell Camille was exhausted.

The detective had spoken with Camille several times since they had arrived at the station—gently prodding her for any information about what had happened that night and where Art might be. Camille had continued to insist that she knew nothing—that Art hadn't told her anything about where he was going or what he was doing. Mary was relieved to have her daughter back safe and sound. But Art was still out there somewhere—and that worried her.

Detective Evans stuck her head into the room. She looked as worn-out as Mary felt.

"No sense in keeping you here," the detective said. "Let me grab my coat, and I'll drive you home."

"Thank you," said Mary. "You'll call if anything happens?"

"Of course," said the detective. "And you'll let me know if Camille remembers anything?"

"Of course," replied Mary.

The worried mother reached over and shook her daughter's shoulder. "Let's go home," she said gently.

The little voice in her head told her to wake up, but her body resisted.

Camille was warm and comfortable. And it felt good.

The voices around her were indistinct, distant, unintelligible — like the adult voices in a Charlie Brown cartoon.

"Just another five minutes," she murmured.

The distant voice became slightly clearer. "It's late," the voice said.

It was her mother's voice.

"Just another five minutes," Camille said again out of pure instinct.

"We need to go," her mother said.

"Just another . . ." the girl started to say again — but the little voice in her head suddenly screamed at her to wake up.

Camille shot up instantly from the couch.

"What time is it?" she asked in a panic.

Detective Evans checked her watch. "Just a bit after

midnight," she said. "You've been asleep for a good hour or so."

"Oh no," replied Camille. "No, no, no."

She reached into her pocket and pulled out the folded-up piece of paper that Art had given her.

She was too late.

CHAPTER 46

12:04 a.m.
Sunday, December 17
West Building, National Gallery of Art,
Washington, DC

There are a lot of important paintings at the National Gallery of Art in Washington, DC.

The walls are filled with paintings by Claude Monet, Edouard Manet, Rembrandt van Rijn, and Raphael.

Works by El Greco.

Johannes Vermeer.

Sandro Botticelli.

Mary Cassatt.

They are history's greatest painters, and they produced some of the world's most famous paintings.

But there is only one painting by Leonardo da Vinci at the National Gallery of Art.

It is a portrait of a young aristocrat by the name of Ginevra de' Benci, a woman of renowned beauty and the inspiration for many poems in her lifetime.

In fact, it is the only painting by Leonardo da Vinci on view in a museum in the United States.

The painting resides in Gallery 6 on the main floor of the West Building of the National Gallery of Art. It is mounted on a stand in the middle of the room. A single spotlight shines down on it. The walls of this particular gallery are the thickest in the museum. There are no windows. There is one doorway that serves as both entrance and exit. It is a literal dead end. And it is also where Arthur Hamilton Jr. had decided to rescue his father.

Slightly out of breath from his quick journey through the ventilation system and across several galleries, Art crouched down behind the stand and waited.

Dr. Roger Belette led the way to Gallery 6.

Arthur Hamilton listened as Belette explained the history of the painting to Palmer, who did not seem the least bit interested. Hamilton suspected that his son's selection of this particular painting was not random. The portrait of Ginevra de' Benci by Leonardo da Vinci has one particularly unique feature—the painting is two-sided. On the reverse side of the wooden panel on which the portrait is painted is a wreath of juniper, laurel, and palm and the poet's motto. In normal circumstances the back of a painting is rarely seen —a painting may sit flat against a wall for decades, if not centuries. The inscription on the back of the painting of Ginevra would have been known only to a select few—a secret to the rest of the world. Today, though, the painting is displayed so that both the back and the front can be seen. And the connection between the portrait by Leonardo da Vinci and the water stain on the back of the fake van Gogh was unmistakable.

As proud as he may have been of what his son was trying to do, Hamilton also knew that they would be lucky to survive the night. Art should have called the police. He should have protected himself. Art had allowed his emotions to get the better of him.

Hamilton hoped that his son had some sort of plan.

"We're here," Belette said.

Hamilton, Palmer, and Belette stood just outside the entrance to Gallery 6. Palmer's two thugs remained close behind. In the middle of the dark room and highlighted by a single spotlight was a small square painting on a tall stand— only fifteen inches by fifteen inches in size. A brass railing surrounded the painting. The young woman on the canvas gazed out at the viewer with a stoic look on her face. It was Ginevra, the aristocrat. The painting hinted at da Vinci's more famous work— *La Gioconda*, or, as it is more commonly known, the *Mona Lisa*.

"Is there another entrance to the room?" asked Palmer.

Belette shook his head. "No," he said. "It's the most secure room in the museum— and for good reason. One way in, and one way out."

Palmer smiled and stepped into the room, followed by

Belette and Hamilton. Hamilton looked around for any sign of his son, but the small room appeared empty.

"Enough games," Palmer announced loudly. "No more riddles, clues, or notes. I want the journal, and I want it now."

The room was silent for what seemed like an eternity. Hamilton hoped that his son had thought better of whatever plan he might have had. But then, suddenly, a voice came out of the darkness.

"Do we have a deal?" the voice asked.

It was Art's voice. Hamilton's heart dropped in his chest. They were trapped.

The boy appeared from behind the stand that held the da Vinci painting. He clutched the journal in his right hand.

"Art!" Hamilton exclaimed, and started for his son.

One of Palmer's subordinates grabbed the father by his arm and stopped him in his tracks. Hamilton winced in pain.

"Hand over the journal," Palmer said.

"Let my dad go," said Art, "and you can have it."

Palmer laughed. "In case you haven't noticed," he said, "you're no longer in a position to negotiate. This is checkmate. So no more games—hand over the journal."

Art did not immediately respond. He simply stood in place and stared across the room.

"Fine," he finally said. "You can have it."

The boy tossed the journal at Palmer. It hit the floor and slid to a stop just short of Palmer's feet.

Palmer picked up the journal and started thumbing through it.

"It's on the tabbed page," said Art.

Palmer turned to the page with the small yellow tab and examined the drawings. "The spider," he said appreciatively. "We have been looking for you, my little friend."

Palmer handed the journal to Belette. "Destroy it," he said. "Leave nothing but ashes."

Belette nodded and mumbled that he would take care of it immediately.

"I've kept my part of the deal," said Art. "Now let my dad go."

Palmer smiled. "You didn't really think that would happen, did you?"

"But we made a deal," Art pleaded. "You've got what you need."

"That's correct," replied Palmer. "I have everything I need."

Palmer turned to one of the large men with him, the one with the thick glasses. "Grab the boy," he instructed.

"Wait!" said Hamilton. "Please." He turned to Palmer. "Let me talk to my son," he said. "He'll cooperate, I promise. I don't want this to be any harder than it needs to be."

"Fine," Palmer said. "Make sure he cooperates. One

wrong move from either you or your son, and we'll end this here and now. Understood?"

"Understood," said Hamilton as he wrenched his arm free from Palmer's underling.

Hamilton made his way across the room and stood next to the brass railing directly in front of his son. Tears welled up in the boy's eyes. Hamilton reached down, pulled the boy over to his chest, and hugged him tightly.

"You shouldn't have done this," he whispered to his son. Hamilton could feel the tears welling up in his own eyes. "Listen," he continued to whisper. "When we leave, I'll try to create some sort of distraction. When I do, just run."

"I'm not leaving you again," replied Art firmly.

"There's no other way," said Hamilton.

"There *is* another way," Art said.

"Okay," said Palmer. "Time to go."

He nodded at the man with the thick glasses, who started across the room toward the Hamiltons.

The boy pushed away from his father. "I wouldn't come any closer," the boy said. He locked eyes with Palmer.

Hamilton looked down at his son with a look of surprise on his face.

The boy continued to stare across the room at Palmer.

Bazanov hesitated. He glanced over at his leader.

"Get them, and let's go," said Palmer.

"I wouldn't do that," the boy said. He pulled a small

plastic bag from his pocket and held it up for everyone to see. It contained some sort of red powdery substance.

"And what is that supposed to be?" said Palmer. "A magical potion?"

"Sort of," replied Art. "It's a little mixture I put together. My dad showed me how to do it once when we were in Italy—we made homemade poppers. You know, the little fireworks you throw to the ground and they explode. It was awesome. But my dad made me promise to never do it on my own. He said it was too dangerous."

Arthur Hamilton Sr.'s jaw dropped. "You didn't," he said. "Please tell me you didn't use the potassium chlorate?"

"I did," said the boy. "And this bag is, like, a thousand times bigger than the little poppers we made—it'll be awesome. Red flames and a big explosion."

Lantham, Bazanov, and Belette started to slowly back away, a look of uncertainty on their faces.

"The boy's bluffing," said Palmer. "I can't believe any of you are buying this. If I have to take care of this myself, I will."

Palmer started walking across the room toward Hamilton and his son.

"I wouldn't do that," said Hamilton. "My son doesn't know what he's doing. That stuff can be very unstable. If he mixed it up incorrectly, then the stuff in that bag could blow us all up."

"I *am* a little nervous," said the boy. "And my hands are getting all sweaty."

Lantham, Bazanov, and Belette each took two more steps back. "We still don't know what he did with Nigel," Bazanov muttered. "The kid's some sort of . . . junior attack ninja or something. Maybe he blew Nigel up."

Palmer stood in the middle of the room and waved his arms wildly in the air. "There is nothing in that bag but colored sand or Kool-Aid. I'm telling you, it's a bluff!"

"It's not a bluff," Art said.

And without another word of warning, the boy simply tossed the small plastic bag toward Palmer and the others.

CHAPTER 47

Art watched the bag flip end over end as it flew across the room in the direction of the four men. It reminded him of watching a play in baseball, when a group of infielders converge on a fly ball—no one calls for the catch, and everyone assumes someone else is going to make the play.

But no one caught it. No one made the play. The ball—or rather, the bag—simply fell between all of them as they stood and watched.

The boy had expected to hear some sort of *splat* as the bag hit the ground.

But there was no splat—only a boom. A really big boom.

The bag exploded in a burst of bright red light. Smoke instantly filled the room.

The flash of light and the smoke had left Dorchek Palmer

dazed and struggling to see what was going on around him. His ears were ringing from the explosion, but he could faintly hear Lantham, Bazanov, and Belette coughing and screaming like small children as they desperately tried to make sure all their hands and fingers were intact. Palmer took a step back but tripped over Belette, who had fallen to the floor in the confusion.

"Get them!" Palmer screamed from where he'd landed on the ground. "They can't get away."

There was no more time for games — Palmer knew that he needed to end this mess now. He pulled a gun from his coat and stood back up.

He could see figures moving around in the smoke, but exactly who was doing what was unclear.

Palmer positioned himself near the entrance to the room and prepared to shoot anyone who tried to leave.

Despite everything that was going on around them — the smoke, the yelling, the screaming, the coughing — Arthur Hamilton Sr. could not help but smile.

The blast of light from the explosion and the ensuing smoke had provided the perfect cover for their escape. Art's plan had been brilliant — if more than a little reckless and dangerous.

Arthur Hamilton grabbed his son by the arm. "Let's go," he whispered.

"No," said Art. "We're staying here."

Hamilton couldn't believe what he was hearing. How could they stay? Palmer would not show any mercy — they would not make it out of the room alive.

"But we need to go," insisted Hamilton. "Now!"

Art did not respond. Instead, he tore himself free from his father's grip and stepped over to the painting by Leonardo da Vinci. Art looked at his father for a brief second, then turned back to the artwork.

"What are you doing?" Hamilton exclaimed.

But it was too late. The smoke was already starting to clear — and Hamilton could hear Palmer shouting directions from the far side of the room.

They had missed their opportunity.

And that's when the boy did something totally unexpected. Hamilton watched as his son ripped the five-hundred-year-old fragile and priceless da Vinci painting from its stand.

Dr. Roger Belette, still on the floor, was the first to see it.

The smoke had cleared just enough for him to make out the figure of the boy standing in front of the da Vinci painting in the middle of the room.

The director's jaw dropped as he watched the boy wrench the painting free from the panel.

The first thought that passed through Belette's mind was concern over the painting — he was, after all, the head of acquisitions for the museum, and the boy was manhandling an irreplaceable piece of history. There are only a relatively small number of paintings by Leonardo da Vinci in existence, and the boy was recklessly tearing one of the artist's portraits from the stand on which it was hanging.

Didn't the boy know better?

And then a second thought hit Belette like a speeding train. He understood exactly what the boy was doing.

But it was too late to stop him.

Palmer stood and assessed the situation. Only a thin haze of smoke remained in the room. Lantham, Bazanov, and Belette had finally gotten control of themselves after realizing that all their appendages remained fully intact. Lantham and Bazanov had drawn their guns, and they appeared angry.

Remarkably, Hamilton stood in the exact same place as he had when his son had tossed the bag. His son stood to his left, holding something in his arms. Neither had taken the opportunity — presented by the explosion, the smoke, and the confusion — to escape.

Palmer leveled his gun at Hamilton. "It's over," he said.

And that's when Belette screamed.

"The painting!" Belette yelled. "He removed the painting!"

Palmer turned to Belette, who was sitting on the floor with a look of horror on his face. But Belette wasn't looking at the boy, or the painting. He was staring past Palmer — back toward the entrance to the room.

And that's when Palmer heard it. The rapid *click click* of metal gears accompanied by a swooshing sound. Palmer turned around just in time to hear the clicking sound end with a loud metal clang.

He stared at the entrance to the room—which was now completely blocked by a metal security gate. They were trapped.

CHAPTER 48

12:15 a.m.
Sunday, December 17
West Building, National Gallery of Art,
Washington, DC

Palmer went to the gate and tried to lift it. It wouldn't budge.
Bazanov and Lantham joined in, the veins in Bazanov's thick
neck popping out like cords. The metal structure would not
give. There was no way under, over, or around it.

Palmer turned to Belette. "Open it!" he demanded.

"I can't," Belette said. He looked as if he would throw up
at any moment. "I told you, this is the most secure room in
the museum — that's why the da Vinci is in here. As soon as
the boy removed the painting, the room's security system
was activated and the gate came down. It can't be opened
from inside the room."

Palmer rushed across the room and grabbed Belette by
his collar. "Then who can open it?" he screamed.

"O-only the security st-staff," Belette stammered. "But
they may already be on their way down here. There will be
questions."

"Then I suggest you provide them with answers, and quick," said Palmer.

He turned to Hamilton and Art. His eyes burned with fury. The cool, calm demeanor was gone. "I've spent years planning this," he growled. "The van Gogh forgery was perfect. I will not let one small boy ruin everything."

He leveled his gun at Art.

"I wouldn't do that if I were you," said a voice from behind him.

Palmer turned around. On the opposite side of the gate stood a short woman in a long dark coat. She had short black hair, and a pair of reading glasses hung from a chain around her neck.

Palmer pointed his gun at her. "Open the gate!" he said. "Now!"

The woman removed her right hand from the pocket of her coat and held it up. She was holding a badge. "Detective Brooke Evans of the Metropolitan Police," she said. "And you're under arrest."

Out of the corner of his eye, Palmer saw Belette faint and fall back on the floor with a thud.

"Open the gate!" Palmer demanded once again.

The woman sighed. "As I said," she repeated calmly, "you're under arrest."

"I don't think you understand the situation," said Palmer.

"Nor do you," replied the woman.

Suddenly the corridor outside the gallery was flooded

with police officers and men and women with the letters FBI emblazoned across their chests. They all had guns drawn and pointed at Palmer, Lantham, and Bazanov.

"I suggest you all drop your weapons," said the detective calmly.

"Get the boy and his father," Palmer said to Bazanov and Lantham. "We'll use them as hostages."

"Are you kidding?" said Lantham. Palmer watched as Lantham put his weapon on the floor and placed his hands high over his head. Bazanov glanced once at Palmer, then placed his own weapon on the ground.

Palmer looked around. Belette was flat on his back on the floor, and Bazanov and Lantham stood with their arms raised in surrender. There were at least thirty police officers and FBI agents standing in the corridor outside the gallery.

Dorchek Palmer had nowhere to go.

Years of planning and preparation to commit the perfect crime had all been for nothing—all because of a blond-haired boy who had lost his memory.

It was over, and Palmer knew it.

He put his gun on the floor.

And with that, the metal gate slowly started to rise.

CHAPTER 49

12:47 a.m.
Sunday, December 17
West Building, National Gallery of Art,
Washington, DC

Art and his father sat on a bench in the West Sculpture Hall and watched as the FBI and Metropolitan Police scurried about the museum. The FBI had already escorted Palmer, his henchmen, and Belette from the museum. Detective Evans said it would be only a matter of time before the other people involved were rounded up as well—Belette had made it clear that he would tell the police everything he knew to try to save his own hide. The museum's director stood on the far side of the hall speaking with Detective Evans and an FBI agent. She appeared to be in shock at what had taken place in her museum and directly under her nose.

"They almost did it," said Art. "One hundred and eighty-three million dollars."

Art's father shook his head. "One hundred and eighty-three million?" he said. "This isn't about one hundred and eighty-three million dollars. Try two, maybe three, billion dollars."

"What?" Art exclaimed. "How is that even possible?"

"The van Gogh was just the start," replied his father. "The fake painting was supposedly part of a lost collection of paintings hidden away for years in a vault in Berlin."

"Why would anyone believe the story about the lost collection?" asked Art. "It seems so . . . well, fake."

"It was fake, but they believe it because of men like Hildebrand Gurlitt."

"Who?" Art was well versed in art history, but that particular name did not ring a bell. He wondered if the amnesia was still affecting him.

"Gurlitt was an art dealer who worked with the Nazis during World War II," said Arthur Hamilton. "He secretly put together a collection of more than a thousand paintings that he stole during the war—all of them masterpieces. Nobody—and I mean nobody—knew about the paintings. He didn't try to sell them or show them off. They were all just stuffed into a small cramped apartment. When Gurlitt died, his son took over the apartment—and he didn't tell anyone about the paintings. The secret simply continued."

"So what happened?" asked Art. "Someone eventually found out, right?"

"Eventually," replied his dad, "but only when Gurlitt's son was very old. In fact, when his son died, a painting by

Claude Monet was found in the suitcase he took to the hospital."

"Wow," said Art. He didn't feel quite as bad about tearing the da Vinci from the wooden stand. At least he hadn't stuffed it into a suitcase.

Arthur Hamilton explained that there were still thousands of lost and stolen paintings—masterpieces by Vermeer, Raphael, Manet, da Vinci, Michelangelo, and, yes, Vincent van Gogh.

"So this wasn't just about selling the van Gogh painting," Art's father said. "It was to convince people that the rumored lost collection was real—that they could believe it existed. If the National Gallery of Art bought a painting from that collection, then the rest of the world would soon follow."

"But who would buy all of those paintings? Wouldn't some museum eventually figure it out?"

"Maybe," replied Art's dad. "Or maybe not. The fake van Gogh was really, really good—the best fake I've ever seen. But more important, there's pride involved."

"Pride?"

"Yes, pride. Back in 2012, the Royal Family of Qatar purchased a painting by Paul Cézanne for two hundred and fifty million dollars. There are other countries and people with unimaginable wealth who would line up in a second to buy a masterpiece by Vincent van Gogh, or hundreds of other painters. Trust me, no one wants to believe they paid hundreds of millions of dollars for a fake — so they simply don't ask."

Art sat back and contemplated what might have happened if Palmer's plan had succeeded — hundreds of fake paintings sold for billions of dollars across the globe. And the only thing that had kept that from happening was a small leather journal tucked away in the boy's backpack.

Arthur Hamilton put his hand on his son's shoulder. "And even though what you did was incredibly foolish and dangerous," he said, "I'm very proud of you."

"It wasn't just me," Art replied. "There was this girl named —"

"Art!" a loud voice screamed across the sculpture hall.

All the police officers, detectives, and FBI agents stopped what they were doing and turned in the direction of the sound.

"Art!" the voice screamed again.

Camille was sprinting across the hall, her red hair flying in all directions. "Art! Art!" she screamed as she ran. There was a huge smile on her face.

Arthur Hamilton looked to his son. "Your fan club?" he asked.

"No," Art responded. "My friend."

AUTHOR'S NOTE

In 1888, while living in Arles, France, Vincent van Gogh painted *The Park at Arles with the Entrance Seen Through the Trees.*

Following Vincent's death in July 1890, ownership of the painting passed through a number of hands until it found its way to a private residence in Berlin, Germany, in 1928. Unfortunately, the trail ends in Ber- lin, where the painting was presumably destroyed by fire during World War II. Today, only a black-and-white image of the painting remains. However, in a letter to his brother Theo, Vincent provides some hint of what has been lost to history:

> [N]ature here is extraordinarily beautiful. Everything and every-
> where. The dome of the sky is a wonderful blue, the sun has a pale
> sulphur radiance, and it's soft and charming, like the combination
> of celestial blues and yellows in paintings by Vermeer of Delft. . . .
> But my colours, my canvas, my wallet are completely exhausted
> today. The last painting, done with the last tubes on the last canvas,
> is a naturally green garden, is painted without green as such, with
> nothing but Prussian blue and chrome yellow.[1]

[1]Credit: Van Gogh Museum, Vincent van Gogh: The Letters, Letter 683 to Theo van Gogh. Arles, Tuesday, 18 September 1888.

Still, not all hope is lost—and the underlying premise of *The Van Gogh Deception* remains sound. As recently as 2014, tax collectors in Spain found a van Gogh painting that had been missing for decades in a safety deposit box. Perhaps one day *The Park at Arles with the Entrance Seen Through the Trees* will likewise re-emerge.

A big thanks to Anita Homan, documentalist at the Van Gogh Museum in Amsterdam, for her assistance in tracing the provenance of the painting. And a big thanks as well to Elizabeth Thorne and Katie Forsyth of Brookstone School in Columbus, Georgia, for their assistance with a tricky French translation. *Merci beaucoup.*

As a lawyer, **DERON HICKS** investigates mysteries for a living. He graduated from the University of Georgia with a degree in painting and from Mercer Law School. He lives in Warm Springs, Georgia, with his wife and children. Visit deronhicks.com.

MORE MYSTERIES BY DERON HICKS

Secrets of Shakespeare's Grave
A Junior Library Guild Selection

A Bank Street Best Book

"Fast-paced and cinematic."
—*Kirkus Reviews*

"A fine traditional mystery with a modern sensibility." —*Booklist*

Tower of the Five Orders
A Junior Library Guild Selection

"A pleasure from start to finish."
—*Booklist*

"A spirited follow-up. . . . Boasts intelligent writing." —*School Library Journal*